Praise for Screwing With Perfect

"Screwing with Perfect is worth spending an evening curled up on the sofa... a tender romance filled with a side of erotic, sizzling chemistry. Screwing with Perfect has not only earned 5 Angels but also a Recommended Read!"

~ *Jessica, Fallen Angel Reviews*

"This story is soooo hot! I also love the sexual innuendo woven throughout the story (like the plumbing scene). I'm a big fan of Ms.Trent's work but this is my favorite so far. I was pulled into Kes's and Drew's world and didn't leave till the very last page. I love Ms. Trent's talent for building sexual tension and keeping it tight throughout the story--even after the hero and heroine have sex. This one's on my keeper shelf."

~ *Angela Black, Sensual Romance Reviews.*

5 Stars "A fantastic tale of love blossoming between best friends, Screwing with Perfect was both inspirational and engaging. The dead-on realistic descriptive voice of Ms. Trent brought her characters to life and truly made them memorable. ...With some surprising revelations about their sexual preferences, there was a host of kinky exploration that made for an explicitly hot experience. Screwing with Perfect is a story well worth recommending."

~ *Sin St.Luke, Just Erotic Romance Reviews*

Screwing With Perfect

Louisa Trent

A Samhain Publishing, Ltd. publication.

Samhain Publishing, Ltd.
2932 Ross Clark Circle, #384
Dothan, AL 36301
www.samhainpublishing.com

Editing by Jewell Mason
Cover by Anne Cain

This title has been previously published electronically.
First Samhain Publishing, Ltd. electronic publication: July 2006
First Samhain Publishing, Ltd. print publication: October 2006

Dedication

To My Family

Chapter One

The door to Kesley Richmond's third floor apartment burst in. No knock.

"Overflow," her downstairs neighbor announced, storming her threshold. "My ceiling just sprung a waterfall. A *blue* waterfall," Andrew Chandler added pointedly.

Plunger in hand, he headed for her bathroom down the hall.

A rebel, a renegade, a radical free thinker, Drew rarely, if ever, observed polite niceties, a knock before entering her private space only one of the many customs he totally ignored. When she thought about it, and she did all the time, Kesley couldn't put her finger on a single social convention he observed.

She, on the other hand, was a slave to convention. For example, every month she religiously plunked a blue tablet in her toilet tank—a *major* bone of contention between them, far surpassing the battle of the sexes over the correct protocol for the positioning of the toilet seat when not in use. Naturally, as a female, she strictly adhered to the seat-down imperative.

Drew ascribed to the seat-up, male prerogative.

In the bathroom politic, they held to strict party lines.

As to the custom of blue tablets—well, Drew simply didn't understand their importance in the grand scheme of things. In his nonconformist view of the world, he missed the whole big picture.

"Kes, sweetheart, prettying up the toilet bowl is a waste of time."

That's what he'd *said*, anyway.

Lip service. Only last week, when the water flushed clear right before her company was due to arrive, he'd changed his tune quick enough.

Fresh out of tablets and facing the looming prospect of naked toilet bowlitis in front of her snooty sorority sisters, she'd panicked. After she'd yelled the situation down to Drew on the second floor, he'd raced to the store for her, without her having to ask him. He didn't return with just a single box of blue tablets either. Oh, no, not Drew. He never did things in half-measures. Instead, he'd bought a whole year's supply. Just for her. Just so she wouldn't needlessly suffer the embarrassment of an ugly toilet bowl for the next twelve months. And the blue tablets weren't even on sale!

Not only that, while she'd delayed her college friends from …*ahem*…powdering their noses, Drew crept up the back stairs and dropped one of those "waste of time" tablets in the tank before anyone knew the difference. Afterwards, when she thanked him for his thoughtfulness, he shrugged off the good deed as though it meant nothing, saying he'd only bought "the damn blue urinal cakes" so he wouldn't have to listen to her go on and on about her shortcomings when she had no shortcomings…or words to that effect.

She did tend to obsess at times.

But her somewhat neurotic preoccupation with minute details wasn't the real reason Drew came to her rescue. The *real* reason he came to her rescue was…

Hmm—

She blanked. Completely ran dry on ideas.

Unusual. When it came to human motivation, she never drew blanks.

Frowning, Kesley cocked her head to the side, twirled a lank piece of hair around a finger, and considered Drew's hidden agenda.

She had it!

Drew was still in the closet about those blue tablets. Hate them? Ha! Actually, he *loved* them. Poor self-deluded guy. When would Drew get in touch with his inner self?

She still had hope for him. Someday, with a little prompting, she knew he'd admit to his love. And Drew was the type of person who, once outed, would never return to his old ways.

That resolved, Kesley jumped up from her desk and hotfooted it after him down the hall.

"Sorry about the flood," she called at his wide shoulders. "Can I help?"

"That's okay, sweetheart. I can handle this alone."

"Mind if I watch? I could use a break."

Understatement. Before Drew's arrival, she'd been pouring over the sketchy case history of the newest troubled teen to arrive at The Shelter, where she worked as a social worker. The few details contained within the report were grim and all too familiar. God, what she wouldn't give for a laugh.

The irreverent Drew was always good for a chuckle. Say what she would for his devil-may-care attitude towards life, the man did wonders for lightening her mood.

Drew hiked his stylish gray pleated dress pants up to the knee. "You wanna watch? Watch away. I don't mind voyeurs."

Her downstairs neighbor did display certain exhibitionistic tendencies. However, as much as she needed an infusion of comedy, he offered nothing to laugh about here. She lusted after men with good-looking legs, and Drew's muscled calves made her salivate, not chuckle.

Correction. More than his good-looking legs made her salivate. Everything about Drew was drool-worthy. Tall, even with his chronic slouch. Athletic, though he never appeared to tax himself. And blond, without the enhancement of any hair products. Drew was by far the most naturally attractive man she had ever seen. When they first met, his male beauty had bowled her over, just about left her speechless. This in a woman who prided herself on her effective communication skills.

Ten years later, Drew's male good looks still bowled her over. Fortunately, she had long since recovered her ability to speak in his presence, especially about really *important* issues.

"New shoes?" she asked as he kicked off his loafers.

"Naw. I've had these for years. I like 'em because they don't need tying. Just slip 'em off and on. You know me, Kes, I never do anything extra if I don't have to."

Those extras included the wearing of underwear and socks. Drew never bothered with those either. The lack of socks she had visually confirmed. Going commando—well, that was what he said, anyway.

"Geez, sweetheart," he shot over his shoulder as he waded barefoot across her flooded tile floor, "haven't you read the signs posted in little girls' rooms about the proper disposal of them there things? Flushing 'em clogs up the works."

"Wrong time of the month, pal. So, *them there* things are not causing the overflow. And I never flush 'em," Kesley said, not only defending herself but all of womanhood against the arrogance of male plumbing superiority.

She darted Drew a suspicious look. "And how do you know what's posted inside ladies' restrooms?"

"Direct observation." Drew rolled up his shirtsleeves and got down to the business at hand, namely unplugging the lazy toilet trap.

Kesley had always secretly admired Drew's outrageousness. She harbored no small curiosity herself about what went on inside the opposite sex's restrooms. Like, why was there invariably a line inside the double "X" chromosome door but no waits inside the "XY"? Men were in and out in seconds flat, while women chatted with each other in polite agony until a stall vacated. Rather than wait, many a time she'd wanted to cross the gender barrier and enter that mysterious boys' room door. Naturally, she never did. And here was Drew openly acknowledging he'd taken the daring leap into gender crossing territory. This was one story she had to hear.

She bit her lip in gleeful anticipation. "The ladies inside the restroom— what did they say when you barged in on them?"

"Hey, Kes, I'm no perv. The direct observation happened after hours, during one of my away-from-home consult jobs, when hardly anyone else was around. Only the two of us were in there, her and me." He gave a phony shiver. "Brr. Scary places are women's restrooms." Drew removed the toilet lid, and went in up to the elbow.

"Wait a minute. Don't leave me hanging like this. What were you doing in there with a woman? Do you just randomly offer your plumbing services to anyone and everyone, free of charge?"

Drew glanced over at her, a squinched look of male exasperation making his face all the more gorgeous. "Kes, sweetheart, what do you think I was doing in there with a woman?"

"Oh, *that*."

"Yes, *that*. The men's room didn't have a lock on the door and the women's room did, so we went in there. And for your information, I never offer my—" he paused theatrically, "—*plumbing services* randomly. I have to at least like the woman. And I never charge. A simple thank you is more than sufficient."

"Generous of you."

"I think so," he said loftily.

Same as always, Kesley couldn't tell whether or not Drew was teasing her, but she laughed anyway. God, but laughing felt good.

Startling blue eyes, bluer than even the toilet bowl tablets, twinkled at her. "I consider what I do a public service. In this instance, the woman was a fellow consultant, away from home on her birthday. She was lonely, and I was available." He shrugged. "What the hell? I couldn't very well turn her down. Not on her special day. That would have been heartless. As it was, we had some fun and it didn't mean anything to either of us."

"Could've bought her a cake instead," she grumbled.

"Birthday candles are *so* not what this lady had in mind to blow."

No need to ask what the woman had wished for—Drew was any woman's wish come true. If aware of his effect on the opposite sex, he never acknowledged it. A conceited ass about his sexual prowess, he had no vanity at all about his appearance. He never looked in a mirror and, like everything else, did personal grooming while doing something else. He combed his hair on the fly, shaved perusing the newspaper, brushed his teeth watching the morning sports on TV—done without leaving toothpaste trails on the floor she could later sanctimoniously point to and say, "See those globs? Those globs are the reason you should brush your teeth over the bathroom sink like everybody else!"

But Drew never left globs. He did everything with effortless grace.

The classy guy offered, "A toilet stall's ambience isn't exactly conducive to romance."

"Could've taken her back to your motel room."

"I did, smarty-pants. Afterwards." He shook his head ruefully. "I tell you, I was not up to my usual high standards in that tiny cubicle. Why, I could barely perform."

A first for Drew. The man performed with greater frequency than a jackrabbit on Viagra, or so the stories went.

Leaning a denim-encased hip against the doorjamb, the raised threshold damming the room's wet interior, Kesley offered a not-so-spontaneous aside to Drew's salacious restroom story. "I haven't gone out on a date in over a year."

"What about me?" Drew looked over at her again. "Don't I count? We go out all the time. Last time I looked, I still had all the right working parts. And, I can fix your plumbing too."

Kesley smiled. She was counting on it.

Chapter Two

"Sweetheart, about that plumbing remark…I didn't mean it in a double-entendre sort of way. Honest. I was talking literal. You know, I can fix your broken stuff, do household repairs, like fixing toilets. Not the other thing. Not the sex thing."

"I know," Kesley said quickly, in response to the strained look on Drew's face. Geez. Already she was scaring him off.

"Just so you do." The handyman returned to work, his features relaxing.

Drew never talked sex with her. Oh, he alluded to his escapades with a broad and comical sweep of the brush, but the intimate details stayed blurred. Even so, she knew Drew was everything outside her realm of experience. Then again, just about everything sexual was outside her realm of experience. In school, she'd studied. During work hours, she worked. After work hours, she worked overtime. She always did the appropriate activity for the setting. In bed, for instance, she slept. That was all she did in bed. Ever. Appropriateness was the bane of her existence.

"I meant, I haven't had a *real* date in a year," she corrected, appropriately qualifying her previous statement. "Finding a guy interested in commitment, even one who practices serial monogamy, is just about impossible. Why does a man find having sex with only one woman at a time in any given week so difficult?"

"I can't speak for all men, but I don't do anything just because it's the expected thing. There has to be a reason. A good reason. Look at it this way," he said philosophically, "no commitment means no back-and-forth bickering over who gets custody of the houseplants when the relationship sours. And relationships always eventually sour."

She shook her head. "That's so sad."

"Don't be sad, Kes. I shouldn't have said that. Forget I did. Monogamy is dying out, but it's not extinct yet. Some men are faithful. Some never stray. So don't give up, my girl. Somewhere out there, a guy is waiting just for you. And if he fools around on you, I'll break both his legs and tie his you-know-what in a knot so he can't cheat on you ever again. How's that?"

"A two-timer on a stretcher with a knotted you-know-what. Every woman's dream date."

"We shouldn't be talking about this, Kes," Drew said uneasily.

No, they never talked sex. This didn't mean she'd missed out on the infamous stories, a secondhand re-telling through mutual friends in the know. She'd gained a whole new respect for Drew's ability to multi-task after hearing his adventures with the Monroe triplets. Of course, Donna, Lonna and Sondra happened before he turned thirty. In the last year, he'd mellowed considerably. According to her sources, Drew now stuck to twins.

The ambidextrous expert jiggled something metal in the toilet tank, while juggling a balloon-like object. "Listen, sweetheart, if you want to go out, why don't we take in a movie? Hell, I can fall asleep just about anywhere."

"Thrilling offer."

"That's me. Thrilling to the bone. So what d'ya say?"

"No thanks. I can go to the movies with a girlfriend."

Drew replaced the toilet lid, and fiddled with the handle. "Okay. Dancing then? I can do that. Not fast dances, though. I gotta draw the line somewhere. Real men do not fast dance."

And Drew was a real man, right down to his pluralistic dating tendencies. "Let's drop the subject. I don't know how we got started on this, anyway. Very unfair of me to put you on the spot. I wasn't really hinting around for you to take me out." Nope, she was hinting around for something else, something more intimate than a date.

"Don't let me off the hook too easy. When I put my mind to it, I'm damn scintillating company."

"Scintillating is far too much to ask of you." Was the other thing too much to ask of him, as well? It shouldn't be. Drew did it all the time.

"Not the handle," Drew decided, now practically up to his ankles in overflowing toilet water.

While staring at his blue appendages—feet from the water on the floor, hands and arms from the water in the tank and wondering if that dye would ever come off—she broached another sensitive subject. "Why are we still living in this dump?"

"It's only a toilet, Kes. Silly to flush what we have down the drain because of faulty plumbing—that is, if we could flush, which we most definitely cannot at the moment."

"This involves more than a temperamental toilet. The toilet is symptomatic of deep-seated underlying issues." She wagged her head pensively. "We need to work this through, examine the dynamics, and maybe discover the causal factors of why we hang on in a place that no longer addresses our needs. We might learn something invaluable about ourselves, something we're denying, through processing this."

Drew groaned. "You gonna throw in co-dependency and enabling too? How about closure? Now there's a gem," he said in undisguised disgust. "Listen, I don't want to be processed, Kes. I like my denial. Leave my dynamics the hell alone. And remember our deal. You speak in social work jargon, and I get to talk in the programming language of my choice."

"Oops! Sorry. In plain English, I'm saying we should move. Get a condo somewhere. We can both afford better. Why not take the next big step of adulthood and live someplace that's actually habitable? Now that we both have credit ratings, what's keeping us here?"

"Convenience."

"All over Boston there are convenient condos with plumbing that consistently works."

"Yeah, but I like this place," he hedged.

Once, she had too. Not hedged—she never hedged. She meant, once she had liked the apartment. The run-down three-decker was her first real taste of independence...

Junior year in college she had drawn a high number in her dorm's lottery system. This piece of bad luck cast her into the swelling rank-and-file of Boston's student homeless. With no choice but to seek off-campus housing, she'd stumbled onto this three-family on the outskirts of the increasing gentrified area of Boston known as Jamaica Plain. To help pay the rent, she and four other displaced female friends decided to live together, settling into the top floor of the building. Meanwhile, Drew and four of his college friends, meeting with a similar lottery fate, opted for the second floor. In the eight years since graduation, all their roomies had moved on. To jobs in other cities or states. To shacking up in lust relationships with members of the opposite sex—or with the same sex in the case of Bruce and Freddy. One of her friends and one of Drew's had even gotten married. Not to each other. Heaven forbid! Those two were now simultaneously paying off divorce lawyers and wedding expenses before the gift silverware had a chance to tarnish...

It was a tough, transitory, throwaway world out there, the only constant being indebtedness—college loans, car loans, vacation loans, and the aforementioned wedding cum divorce loans. Having been given the gift of poverty by her parents—a present money can't buy—she'd always understood the meaning of pinching pennies. Her bank account backed her up on this. As far as she knew, Drew was in good shape financially too. Neither of them owned a car or maintained an expensive lifestyle. They could afford better housing! Yet, they stayed on in the same run-down three-decker, stuck in place, living in an undergrad time warp. Why?

"Fuck a duck! Where's the plunger? Where'd I put it?" asked the other remaining survivor of their college life. "This bowl has gotta be jammed. Maybe you flushed the deodorant again?"

"I don't think so." But pointing a finger, she directed him to the plunger anyway, lying in the corner where he had dropped it earlier. At times, Drew could be forgetful. Or, maybe, he just needed to get in touch with himself and his own hidden motivations.

Picking up the plumber's friend, Drew started working the bowl. "Better catch me for that date now, before I wrap up this current work project. Two, maybe three weeks, tops, I'll be on the move again."

Drew the gypsy. He roamed the country, going from one company to the next, assignment-to-assignment, working out computer glitches, fine-tuning applications, troubleshooting small problems lest they turn into big problems.

She sighed. Too bad people couldn't be debugged as easily.

As Drew's arm flexed on the plunger, she took the plunge too. "I've decided to get serious about dating. But it's hard work, you know? All that dead conversational air to fill. I end up telling the same funny anecdotes over-and-over again. I need new joke material."

"Try current events," Drew helpfully suggested.

"I want my date happy, not crushingly depressed. Current events are inappropriate for superficial dating banter. Let's face it, without joke material from you, I'm boring."

"You're not boring, Kes. You're a real interesting person."

So like Drew to boost her flagging spirits. "Thanks. But meeting decent guys is just not easy." She sighed again.

"AA didn't work out?"

"Everyone there was a heavy drinker," she confided.

"And you never touch the stuff."

She nodded. "Exactly!"

"Singles night at the bookstore?"

"Since I do actually *read*, I got caught up in book jackets and totally ignored the prowling non-reading customers. The customers who might have interested me were also reading. It's a vicious circle."

"The 'Net?"

Another helpful suggestion. "Grandfathers and adolescents pretending to be otherwise, with the occasional married man thrown in also pretending to be otherwise. The nicest guy I met turned out to be a lesbian. We're still in contact. A lovely woman, but I really do need a non-detachable penis. Whatever happened to guys who are who they say they are?"

"Clubs?"

"Funny you should mention it—I joined one. Well, not actually a club. More like a group. For the recently divorced and/or widowed. Once a week, we meet in the basement of the library to discuss the trials and tribulations of the single life after being a member of a couple. Tame activities. Mainly talk therapy, some role-playing. The group leader asked me to run a session."

"Figures," he muttered, then did a double take. "Wait a minute, Kes. You've never been married."

"A long term relationship counts."

Dyed blue water splashed out of the bowl as a muscled pair of blond-flecked, tanned arms worked in unison. Drew had worked construction to finance his college education. Though his job had changed, the hard body remained. At the sight of that plunger, forcefully driving and thrusting in and out of the toilet bowl, the sound of wetness and suction reverberating in the small space, Kesley's belly clenched.

"Long-term relationship? Sweetheart, I've known you since college. When did you manage to cram one of those into your busy life of helping others?"

"Never," she replied, wondering why Drew suddenly seemed perturbed, "which meant I had nothing to contribute to the discussion, which meant I either sat there in group like a bump on a log or made someone up, which was where the pretend William came in—he left me for another woman."

"That's lame, giving a pretend jerk a name."

"Don't you see? I had to personalize him before I could visualize him. He wasn't real without a name. How could I discuss the no-good creep without picturing him in my head? The name gave him validation. I told the group William left me for someone younger and prettier."

"Twenty-nine isn't old and you are too pretty. Plenty pretty. If Billy-boy had any balls he never would have left you. You should've said you left him. Why give the little fuck the upper hand?"

"I know the other woman thing is a cliché but it did the trick," she said, appalled at how pathetic it all sounded—and devious too—now that she was telling Drew about the experience. "Everyone in the group believed me. Anyway, after an hour or so of discussion, we break up into small groups and console each other. Then comes the good part. Snack time! That's when we mingle. I met a very nice *non-pretend* man over a butterscotch brownie. Ted. Divorced, one child, joint custody, fair child support payments."

Drew stopped what he was doing and stared at her in concern. "What the hell were you doing eating butterscotch? You know you're not supposed to eat butterscotch! Don't you remember that time we went out for a hot fudge sundae because you were PMSing and you needed a chocolate fix but the ice cream place on Huntington Ave only had butterscotch sauce? I held your head up over this very same toilet while you barfed."

Kesley smiled in memory. "Good times."

"The best fucking times. Does this guy Ted even know you're allergic to butterscotch?"

Why was Drew fixating on butterscotch? And how was poor Ted supposed to know she had some weird allergy thing to butterscotch? As they'd only just met, they shared no past history—

And that just went to explain why dating was such hard work. No verbal shorthand, no frame of reference, no remembering when, meant expending oodles of energy getting to know one another. Not that she didn't have oodles of energy.

Kesley waved her arms wildly. "You're missing the whole point, Drew. As Ted was the one who *brought* the butterscotch brownies, I could hardly refuse to eat one. Besides, he's eligible, looking for a committed relationship and, on top of those fine qualities, he seems to like me."

"I can't believe you joined a bitch-and-cry group," Drew muttered. "Don't you get enough of that touchy-feely shit at work, Kes?"

She did. God, she did. She loved social work, but the job was burning her out. Lately, she felt so drained. Working with troubled street kids was particularly brutal. Defiant, resistant, rebellious against authority—and those were the easy cases. Drugs, prostitution, untreated and ignored health problems compounded homelessness and long histories of familial abuse, neglect and abandonment in runaway teens. Some days she just wanted to gnash her teeth in frustration.

Kesley threw her wildly thrashing arms up in the air. "I'm desperate, all right? I'm at the end of my rope. That's why I joined yet another group. And here I met this nice guy who wants to go out with me and I'm afraid to go out with him because I'm a complete fraud."

"Okay, okay, relax, sweetheart. Deep breath. How's about a brown paper bag or something to breathe into?"

"I have never hyperventilated in my life. However, a stress ball would come in handy right about now."

"Stress ball. Stress ball." Drew stuck the plunger under an arm and patted his pockets. "Don't have one of those. Sorry. Wanna give me a stress-busting squeeze instead?"

Muscled arms open scarecrow wide, Drew forded the blue pond to where she stood at the threshold. Not for the first time, he caught her up in his warm embrace. She didn't even mind that a toilet plunger shared the hug or that he dripped blue water all over her. It seemed apropos, considering the blueness of her mood of late.

"Sorry," she murmured into his broad chest. "I shouldn't take my upset out on you, Drew."

"You just take out whatever you want to take out on me. My fault you got upset in the first place," he said, patting her back with his big blue hands, the suction end of the plunger swinging behind him, the rubber end releasing air and making farty noises. "How very *wude*," he lisped. "Pardon me."

After punching Drew and giggling, Kesley felt so much better.

"I don't want you to feel bad. Not ever," the comedian said soulfully. "One little fib about a long-term relationship does not a complete fraud make."

She lifted her chin. "It does, when that one little fib implies a whole big lot...like I'm experienced." She resettled the top of her head under the strong line of his male-model jaw.

"Everyone exaggerates to a certain extent about sex. I, for example, have never done it with triplets, as the rumors I started would suggest."

"You haven't?"

"No. Of course not. I'm not nearly that well coordinated. I'm not even coordinated enough for twins. Forget the ladies' room story too. Never happened. I did buy the woman a cake. Well, okay, it was really a cupcake, but that's a small cake, right? She didn't mind that there wasn't nearly enough space on top for the fifty candles."

"She was *fifty*?"

"If a day. Personally, I think she was closer to retirement age and getting a year older flipped her out. That's what I mean about exaggeration—people exaggerate about themselves all the time and not just about sex. Except you. You're no fraud, Kes. You're the real deal."

"I am too a fraud. As to you—you're not helping me here." And that was *so* not like Drew. He might joke around, never take things too seriously, and his sense of humor was really whacked at times, but when the chips were down, he was always there for her.

"Don't you see? I'm not experienced at all," she told him straight out. "That's why I'm afraid to date Ted, though he's a nice and eligible guy."

"B-b-but Kes, you gotta have *some* experience. Even nice girls have some sex under their belt."

"Get a look at my jeans, pal. See anything in the loops? I don't wear a belt, Drew. And I have no sexual experience. None. I'm a virgin. So how about it? You want to get me up to speed so I can date Ted?"

The plunger dropped out from under Drew's armpit and sank with a blue splash into the pond on the floor. "Well, suck my dick!"

"Fine. That's as good a place as any to start," she replied in relief.

Chapter Three

The next day it poured. Not just a fine drizzle or intermittent sprinkles either. Nope. Buckets. Since his sweetheart refused to believe that sometimes clouds prevail over sunshine, Drew trotted his ass down to the trolley stop to meet her after work, one mother of a raggedy-with-use umbrella in hand. Unlike the optimistic Kes, he brandished the raingear at the first hint of moisture in the air.

While he waited for the streetcar to clickety-clack its way down Huntington Avenue, in his mind's eye, he saw Kes and her "nice guy." They were together. In bed. She languished on top, a black peek-a-boo-lace number draped to her curves. Ted wore lounging pajamas tied loosely around his love handles, butt-crack prominently displayed. In an irritating, dream-sequence kind of slow motion, Ted's soft, pudgy hands reached out to paw Kes. Drew could practically smell the reek of the guy's cologne, could almost see his slicked-back oiled hair. In his dark imaginings, Drew rushed the room, grabbed Kes off the bed, buried his fist in Ted's jowls, and kicked the chump's wide butt out the door.

That's all Drew planned on doing, he swore.

Until—

In the daydream, Kes sort of stumbled and he sort of caught her against him and the strap of her black lacy number sort of fell off her shoulder, and they sort of ended up back in the bed somehow, and what the hell, he kissed her, and damn, one thing led to another, and before he knew it…*damn*. Like any good fantasy, awake or otherwise, soon they were rolling around together—

Drew didn't go any further.

This was *Kesley* he was having dirty thoughts about. The woman was a saint. What she did for those screwed-up kids at The Shelter was over and above the call of duty. Why, she practically lived there. Kes was a good woman, and she deserved all the good stuff in life.

Just that…the thing of it was…Drew had a bad feeling about Ted. Kes understood the human psyche, so why didn't she get that a recently divorced guy equals a guy on the look-out for a good time? Christ, coming off marriage, the poor bastard probably hadn't gotten any in years, so naturally he was on the make. Why didn't Kes understand how men really thought?

Because she had no hands-on experience, that's why.

Drew needed to lay it on the line for her, and in graphic terms, so she'd comprehend what guys like Ted were after. Nice guy Ted wasn't looking for a commitment. He was looking to do the nasty with as many women as he could get in the sackeroo.

The trolley brake pads screeched, and the double doors folded back. Kes came into view, wisps of short brown hair blowing across her beautiful, wholesome face.

Smiling, Kes came towards him. Never one to beat around the bush, she asked, "What are you doing here?"

Reasonable question. "It's raining, and you forgot your umbrella," he said, and tucked her into his side. "Whereas I never forget mine."

"Babe magnet?"

"Nothing better. Get a woman when she's wet and vulnerable, and then cover her quick. That's my modus operandi."

"Smooth," Kes replied and, as he hoped would happen, she laughed.

His sweetheart laughed soft and low, and kind of throatily. A bedroom laugh, if ever he'd heard one. And, he had heard quite a few bedroom laughs in his illustrious career.

Because of the driving rain, they walked companionably close. Her very nice breasts rubbed against his side. Not his fault, because, hey, that was his umbrella arm, which he had to raise to keep her dry. They had walked close before, hundreds of times. They hugged, they always kissed goodbye when he left town, but this was, honest to Christ, the only time he'd ever been conscious of the round firmness of her breasts beyond the basics. Which, was to say, he was a guy, he liked breasts, and hers were nice. Nothing beyond that. But since she'd plunked her virginity in his lap, so to speak, he had begun to speculate about them.

This made him uncomfortable.

Walking all friendly-like with Kes tucked into his side would never be the same again. The mention of sex had already spoiled things between them. Why did she have to go and bring up the subject, anyway? Wasn't getting along enough? They had so much of the good stuff. Why'd she have to go and louse up the perfect relationship with sex? Couldn't she have pretended he was her gay best friend or something? Every woman seemed to have a gay best friend nowadays. He could have been hers. Only he preferred doing it with women, not men. That was the only difference. Oh, and his décor taste was up his ass. He wasn't real great in the clothes department either. Good thing Kes picked out his wardrobe.

Big deal, so he didn't know brand names or how to arrange flowers. He was good at other things, like fixing toilets. And, he was good at loving her. Had always loved her. Since the day they'd first met. Loving Kes was the one constant in his nomadic life.

Kes was tiny, he was not, and so she had to crane her neck up at him whenever she spoke. As his sweetheart was big on talking, he feared for the alignment of her spine.

Drew automatically went into a slouch.

"You know," said she, "when you're on a job halfway across the country, Boston still gets rain."

Huh? What was up with Kes and the weather advisory? Had she stuck one of those hidden messages somewhere in that meteorological report? After years of telling things straight out, had Kes suddenly decided to go symbolic on him?

He'd never know unless he asked. "Uh—sweetie—what's that supposed to mean?"

"It means, when you're not around and it rains and I forget my umbrella, I get wet. And I survive."

Drew frowned, definitely not liking this. Kes sounded testy, like she was trying to prove something. What? What was she getting at?

He had always understood her before. Bring sex into perfection, and everything gets screwed up, logic included.

"I know," he replied. Though, fuck, who was he fooling? He had not a clue.

"And when my toilet overflows," she continued, "I either fix the problem myself or call Mrs. Harris, who in turn calls the plumber."

His frown deepened. What, now he was expendable? Is that what she was saying? He couldn't arrange flowers, didn't know a designer leather handbag from a faux knock-off, and now she didn't need him to fix her toilet?

This was about Ted. Man, he hated that scheming prick. The guy was running a mind scam on Kes, just so he could get his dick up her—

Nope. Wasn't going there. No thinking anatomy when it came to Kes. Saints do not have body parts.

Drew took the high road. "If you're trying to tell me you're a self-sufficient, independent career woman who doesn't need a man around to fix leaking toilets or hold umbrellas, save your breath. I get it. But I'm here now. And I like doing little things for you."

"Oh, yeah? What about the dick-sucking?"

Okay, how contrary was this? When he needed Kes to beat around the bush, she suddenly dropped the symbolism and went back to telling it straight. He was getting dizzy just trying to stay oriented.

This was the deal—in terms of sexual quid pro quo, a BJ was right at the top of the "Something a Woman Does for a Man List" whereas, he was talking "Something a Man Does for a Woman List"—like umbrella carrying.

He tried again. "Dick-sucking—that's not a little thing, Kes. If you saw the size of my dick, you would understand it's not a little thing."

"Oh, yeah? Prove it."

Why couldn't Kes leave sleeping coc—dogs alone? Why couldn't she accept he liked doing little things for her? The hobby went way back, a pleasurable pursuit that started when they first began living together.

Over-exaggeration there, with some creative license thrown in for good measure. They didn't exactly *live together*, live together. He had never *lived* with a woman. They rented different flats in the same three-decker. For the past ten years, it had been his privilege to share the same front staircase, the same communal hallway, the same very-much-present, always-snoopy first-floor landlady, Mrs. Juanita Harris, with Kes, a girl-in-a-million. They had a great set-up going too. His sweetheart took care of his plants and mail while he was away, and he had someone to call and ask about said plants and mail while he was gone. Then, when he was home, he tried to return the favor by doing little things for her—like meeting her at the trolley stop with an umbrella on gloomy days. The arrangement worked out swell. At least, he thought so. So, why the uncharacteristic twinge of resentment coloring her voice—what was up with that?

Sex. The fact she had offered to suck his dick. The fact that she had offered to swallow his—

Nope. Wasn't going there. The woman was a saint. Women like Kes did not do those sorts of things. Making him chicken soup when he came down with a cold, now *that* was a nice woman's thoughtful gesture. But going down on him? That was…that was…

Wrong. So wrong.

His dick did not agree.

The twitch in his pants notched up to semi-firmness. Her mouth took the hit for that.

Kes had these really fine lips. Kind of full. Definitely soft, which he knew from kissing her goodbye. He always zoomed in on them then. Getting to kiss

Kes was the best part of leaving. Sometimes, he only took a job as an excuse to lock lips with her.

But kissing was different than fucking. Way different. In a kiss, he could keep his tongue clear of her mouth, but if they fucked, no fucking way could he keep his dick clear of her—

Nope. Not going there. Absolutely not. Saints do not have one of those.

Just like always, Drew walked Kes up the three flights of stairs, got the door, and followed her inside the apartment. "Run in and take a hot shower, sweetheart, while I start dinner."

When working at his home base in Boston, he spent more time in her place than in his own, his place being neglected—except for the plants—and her place being warm and inviting, lived-in. Since her roommates moved out, he had the run of her apartment. If they had sex, that would probably change. Fucking would just fuck up everything.

While Kes showered, Drew threw a steak on the broiler, and popped potatoes in the microwave for nuking—he'd tossed a salad together before leaving late for work that day. What the hell, he owned the consulting business, and he could come and go as he pleased, travel or not travel. As the boss, he made his own decisions.

Grabbing a cold one from the fridge, Drew made himself at home in front of the tube for the evening news.

When the water in the shower shut off unexpectedly—Kes took l-o-n-g showers—Drew glanced up from the sports to see Kes racing from the bathroom, arms waving at a billowing gray cloud.

"Fire!" she yelled

Shit. Alternating between cheers and swears and jeers at the Red Sox recap, he'd forgotten all about the damn steak.

He beat Kes to the kitchen, shut off the broiler, dumped a box of baking soda on the electrical flames, and swept the cremated cow remains onto a plate. Heaving open a window, he sent the ashy evidence of his absentmindedness into the atmosphere before Mrs. Harris dialed 9-1-1 to put out his faulty memory.

The danger of smoke inhalation over, he looked down at Kes, who appeared alarmingly tiny because she was in bare feet instead of her usual nose-bleed heels.

Rather than run out of the shower naked or wearing a towel, she had grabbed the bed wear she always kept on the inside bathroom door hook. Though the tee was mostly on, t'weren't covering nuthin'. The thin white cotton clung to her damp body and a lot of moist skin was showing.

This was where things got dicey. This was where sex reared its nasty head.

Before, if he had interrupted Kes in the middle of getting changed, which, by the way, he had done many a time because of their friendly open-door policy, he would have quickly averted his eyes to spare them both embarrassment. But things had changed, and now he saw Kes through the tunnel vision of a prospective lover. Assessing. Curious. So how *would* she be in bed, anyway?

Drew worked his way down the moist cotton tee, his eyes caressing womanly curves.

He already knew about the breasts. But the nipples—hey, now there was a pleasant surprise. Bigger than what he had expected, sticking out under the clinging tee, and obviously pink, which made sense because of her light complexion. Kes never went braless, except to bed, a situation he had always before pretended not to notice when he caught her in her jammies. Now he was noticing, openly noticing.

Nice tits, he thought.

He liked tits. They were lots of fun to play with.

His gaze dipping, Drew took the rest of the tour.

Pussy.

Kesley's pussy.

Hmm. Not waxed.

Kes just wasn't the type to tamper with Mother Nature, so a neat patch of light brown curls snuggled under the nearly transparent tee.

He wished he could make out the lips. Were her pussy lips as soft as her mouth? Would they taste just as sweet to kiss? He loved kissing pussy.

Kes was tiny, but she still had legs, shapely legs from all those runs around Jamaica Pond. When he was home, he joined her. Exercise and he did not agree, but he didn't like the idea of his sweetheart running alone.

Nice firm thighs, he mused.

The kind of thighs that could handle a large man like him, that could cradle him in their delta, lock around him as he surged upwards. He knew her body would welcome his body in a way his body had never been welcomed anywhere before. He just knew it. Had always known she'd be perfect for him.

This explained why he never went there, not even in his thoughts. Because after they ended, what then?

He might never see her again, and not seeing Kes would kill him. Better not to have sex at all, than risk losing her for good.

Kes started pulling at the hem of the tee—she must have caught him looking. What the hell did she think he would do after she'd thrown sex in his face?

Sex in his face, sex in his face, he wanted Kes' sex in his face.

"Looks like the tee shirt is winning," he said, walking towards her. "Can I help?"

She groaned. "Drat! I just bought this nightie the other day. I knew I should have gone with the larger size."

"New, huh?" He tugged on the bottom of the clinging cotton, his knuckles scraping her upper thighs.

Knowing where his eyes had been, she blushed and said, "I bought the tee for Ted. For when he stays over."

The prick was staying over? What? On the first date? Saints don't do stuff like that!

She smoothed the cotton over the gravity-defying slope of a tit. "I didn't want to wear something new to bed. So obvious, you know? I thought I'd break the tee in first."

He was going nuts! She was talking about the tee while touching her tit while talking about Ted while he was imagining breaking something in, about breaking Kes in, about breaking her cherry. He had to leave. Had to go. Had to get the hell out of here.

Once covered, Kes shook out her cap of brown hair, sending water drips scattering onto the kitchen floor.

"Careful," he said. "Don't slip. The floor is wet." Losing it, totally going crazy, he blurted, "You're wet too."

What was he saying? What was he doing? Had he just done the unspeakable, told his best bud Kes she was wet?

That did it. Screw this! He definitely had to blow this scene "You know, Kes, I was talking about wet from the shower. Not from the other thing. Not from the sex thing."

Edgy, flustered, frustrated, horny as hell, his sanity slipping away, needing an excuse, any excuse to break the tension, Drew backed up to the bathroom. "I'll just get a towel to dry you off."

Though he had never dried a woman off after a shower, he did like pampering women—

Hell, he just liked women. Their softness, their special scent, their fragility. Their bodies. Burying himself deep inside their bodies. Once. Maybe twice. Before moving on. No hard feelings, moving on was just the way it was.

Which explained why he had never dried a woman off after a shower— he wasn't around long enough for showers.

"You're so tiny," Drew told Kes, moving in on her, towel in hand. "I can stand behind you like this, and see clear across the room."

"I'm not wearing heels, that's why."

He nodded. "Women generally don't wear heels in the shower."

She sighed. "I would if I could. I'd wear heels everywhere—I always wanted a couple more inches."

"Me too. Then, I'd have a full foot to work with."

Kes turned around and gaped. "You mean—?"

"Yup. Didn't I tell you it wasn't a little thing? Sometimes, I don't even have to be in the same room with a lady."

Chapter Four

Turning back around, his sweetheart let that last joke pass. Both too aware of the other for humor, neither of them laughed.

It was the whole sex thing again. His timing was off, and timing was everything in the delivery of a joke. Who invented sex anyway? Sex sucked.

Drew cleared his throat of lust. "Have you thought about birth control?"

"Of course I have! You know I'm not irresponsible. What's gotten into you any way?"

He spun her 'round to face him. "You know damn well what's gotten into me. You've gotten into me."

Her hands went to her hips and the tee shirt tightened across her chest, the move making the hem ride up her thighs again, until he could see her soft brown triangle peeping out. Again. "Why are you growling at me?"

How naïve could she get anyway? Her…her…*area*, for crissakes, was looking him in the eye, his *one* eye. That's why he was growling.

He cleared the lust from his throat. Again. "What are you using?"

"Um—well—*things*."

"You always back the stuff up with a condom. Even if you're deep-throating, make him suit up first."

"I'll go one better than that. When I go downtown, I'm making him wear a tux."

"Balls to the walls, Kes, this is not a laughing matter. As a social worker, you know what's out there."

"I'm fully aware. That's why I need a little happiness, Drew."

He didn't let up. "You plan on doing everything?"

"I never thought about specifics. I don't know."

"Stick to the missionary. No toys. No kink. Vanilla."

"I will not!"

"All guys will try for anal. Back-dooring is the latest Eagle Scout badge. Some will ask, others will insist. You don't give it unless you trust him, and you don't trust him if he tries to wheedle it out of you. That goes for everything. Don't give anything you're not ready to give. Got that?"

"What is your problem?"

"How's Ted?" he asked, testy with the dawn of arousal. "Did you see him today, talk phone sex with him today?"

"Now I know why you're acting strange. You're just miffed because I asked you to deflower me."

He started to laugh. "Deflower? What are you, a Victorian heroine in a romance novel?" he asked, bad humor turned pretty ugly.

She looked down at her bare feet. Wiggled her toes. "I didn't know how else to phrase it."

Drew did. He had a bunch of colorful ways to put the concept into words, but he'd bite off his tongue before using any of them in front of Kes.

"So will you help me?" she asked, gaze still on the floor.

He wound a strand of wet brown hair around a finger, pulled up until he raised her chin, and then bent his jaw to the soft point. When their faces were scant inches apart, he ran a fingertip over her generous mouth. "You're asking me to have sex with you. Right?"

"In a manner of speaking." Her brow puckered. "Well, I suppose so. But really, I was looking at this more from an academic point of view. You have certain knowledge I require and I would like you to facilitate the exchange of that information."

"The facilitation," he said, pronouncing that "f" word with harsh emphasis, much as he would the other, more descriptive "f" word, "will change things between us."

"No it won't."

It already had, goddammit. The fact that Kes had lush, kissable lips had never occurred to him before her request. The way she smelled, sweet and fresh after her shower, had never entered his head. He had never before considered how her petite stature would translate into bed positioning. He liked being with her, but he never once thought about being inside her—

Though sleeping with her, cuddled under the covers with her, had crossed his mind, once or twice, or a million or so times, but the thought wasn't sexual. Nothing sexual. Not with Saint Kesley. She had a whole world out there to save and he didn't want to stand in her way.

His mouth twisted. "I understand you want experience but I just don't know if I can get physical with you."

"Why?"

She was so fucking innocent. "Because I've only ever had sex with strangers. You and me? We're not exactly strangers."

They weren't exactly intimates either. And he'd purposefully kept her out of his head in regards to a lot of speculative stuff.

"Anyway, this is a big step." His mouth dipped to her quivering mouth, and got stuck before touching down. "Suppose we don't click?" he asked, knowing damn well that they would click, and in a big way.

She went up on tiptoes. "That's the beauty of doing this with you. We don't have to click. I only need to click with Ted. It would probably work out better if you and I don't click."

Their mouths were so close. *Help!* He wanted to kiss her.

"H-how was work today?" he asked, a millimeter from her puckered lips.

The corner of that lush mouth twitched. "Lousy. We got a new runaway in. Swears he's eighteen, looks no older than fourteen. He's been living on the streets, and the john who picked him up beat him severely. The kid won't give his real name, won't ask for help, won't accept a helping hand. His stoicism rips me up inside, you know?"

"Aw, Kes—" he said, wanting to fold her in his arms as he would have done before, but not being able to do it now because sex had messed up everything. "I should go."

She touched his shoulder. "You can't run away forever."

When her damp, cotton-covered tit poked his forearm, his cock just about broke through his metal zipper. "Believe me, I know you're here," he said grimly, eye-balling the distance to the door in case he needed to make a break for it.

"You haven't answered my question."

"Don't push me, Kes. I'm thinking." A sprint should get him out of the apartment in under thirty seconds.

"Could you at least look at me while you're thinking?"

He looked. A hard look he never used with her. A challenging look meant to scare her off. He wanted to scare her off because her offer was too tempting to refuse.

The thing was—Kes didn't scare easy. She'd seen so much bad stuff with her compassionate brown eyes, yet somehow always stayed her ground, remaining cheery despite the odds. Like about the onset of rainy weather. It wasn't so much that she denied the clouds, as it was that she hoped the clouds would move on and the sun would shine through.

And that was some foolhardy thinking. Clouds always moved in, not out. And it never just rained, it poured. And an umbrella always came in handy, if not for warding off the deluge, for beating off the muggers hiding behind every bush—those bushes she refused to beat around.

Why didn't Kes carry the can of mace he'd bought for her, that he reminded her to carry like a thousand times? Why wasn't she more careful walking around the city streets? Why was she hopeful despite all the signs against hope?

"Why haven't you taken care of your cherry before now?" he exploded.

"Ending my virginity is not like going to the dentist," she said softly. "The opportunity never presented itself. At least not with the right man."

"And Ted is the right man?"

She blinked. "Ted? Oh! *Ted.* I don't know. Maybe."

"You're going through a lot of bother for a maybe."

"I'll never know unless I try. I'm almost thirty, Drew. It's time. If Ted isn't the right one, some other man will be. I want to get married."

"Swell."

"Please." She tugged on his shirt, like a little girl. "Pretty please? Do this one thing for me and I'll never ask you for another favor as long as I live."

The tip of her pebble-hard tit stabbed him.

Kes was excited, he acknowledged in despair. "I'd do anything for you, but I don't know if I can do this." He grasped at straws. "Here's an idea. Explain the situation to Ted. Just tell him you're a vir-vir—"

"You can't even say it!"

"I can too say it. Virgin," he yelled like a maniac. "See? I said it. There! Aw, hell. Just tell Ted to back off."

"I don't want him to back off."

"Shit!"

"I know what men say about women like me, thirty-year-old virgins. We're the butt of locker room jokes. I'm tired of being a jock's butt."

He tore his hands through his hair. "All right. All right. Just don't tell the pri—Ted. Maybe he won't notice."

"Of course he'll notice! I'm a *virgin.* Haven't you been listening to me?"

"Maybe you lost it already and you just forgot."

"I think I'd remember something like that."

"That's not what I meant. Sweetheart, how many times have you told me about scrapes you got into as a kid?"

"See? I am boring. I repeat the same anecdotes from my childhood."

"I enjoy listening to those stories."

"If you enjoy listening so much, why don't you ever tell one or two of your own?"

Now, instead of her tit poking him in the arm, her finger did. "Huh?" she said, sounding really pissed. "Sometimes I don't think you even had a childhood. You never talk about your folks or anything else."

"Kes, we're getting off the subject here. All's I was trying to say is this— you were a tomboy as a kid. Could be you already busted your cherry climbing trees or whatever."

"You know, sex is not too cool for a woman her first time," she said, completely missing his point. "I don't want to inflict that ordeal on Ted. We don't know each other well enough for me to impose upon him that way. I need someone I'm comfortable with for that."

If you don't know each other that well then maybe you shouldn't be sexing it up, he wanted to holler.

But seeing he had some experience with anonymous fornication himself, only a hypocrite would make that argument. And he was no hypocrite—he was a thirty-year-old single guy who played around. Hell, he liked playing around. No, he *loved* playing around. Playing around was great. He lived, lived, *lived* for sex. And maybe he embellished some of the stories as he related them to his friends—okay, maybe he jazzed them up to the degree that the exploits were no longer recognizable—still, no matter how he cut it, there had been women. And now here was Kes, his little innocent sweetheart, looking to him, the King of Slut, for sexual guidance. Jesus give him strength, because surer than death and taxes, she had come to the wrong man.

But who was the right man? Who should she go to, if not him? More importantly, who should she come for?

Ted?

Drew felt like puking. Kes was too fine a lady to lay it all on the line for that rebounding dick.

Another guy, then?

Drew *guessed* so.

Pulling himself together, Drew tried to reason with her again. "When a woman loses her virginity it should be the most romantic night of her life. The night should be special, a night she'll remember forever. Soft music, soft lights, soft words. A fantasy kind of night. With a lot of shared laughter thrown in, too."

"Cow patties," she scoffed, figuratively assigning his grandiose speech to a pile of B.S. "I don't believe any virgins laughed their way through their first time with you."

"I wouldn't know."

Her brows shot up to outer space. "What?"

"I wasn't there with any of them, Kes. I don't do virgins. Save your first time for the man you love. You'll be glad you did."

Kes rubbed her arms. "I'm tired of saving myself. I'm getting stale saving myself. I'm not a cold woman," she said, looking hotly into his eyes.

"I know."

Drew understood how Kes thought. He knew which movies made her weepy. He knew all about the mushy romances she snuck in the checkout along with the groceries. He had a good idea of what would turn her on. But could he do it?

And how, he could do it!

It was the stopping part that had him worried.

"Okay," he said, his throat tight. "I'll do it."

She drummed her fingers on her lips, all business, all plans. "You leave in two weeks or so. Will that give you enough time to get me up to speed?"

"Once is sufficient to get the job done."

She went on as if she didn't hear him. "There are certain things I'll need to explore. Positions, naturally. Techniques. And then there's the kink factor. I will *not* confine myself to missionary or vanilla. I want inappropriate."

These days, all Drew ever did was the weird stuff. No one on the dating circuit did mom-and-pop sex anymore. Anal was real big, as were bondage and various toys, and triangles and square configurations. Hell, even hexagons were in.

"Yeah, I can do kink." He was tired of it, though. Tired of tying his dates up, tired of lubing them up, tired of making small talk with a crowd in bed.

Occasionally, for a change of pace, he wanted some old-fashioned retro sex where he was alone with the woman, they were looking at each other during the act, and there wasn't a new fashionable fetish to cater to. Just two naked people in bed doing something that felt human, not like a choreographed theatre production.

Kes rolled right along with her grocery list. "And then there are the dead giveaways that might possibly tip Ted off to my lack of experience. I've never slept with a man, so I'll need to get used to an extra set of elbows and knees. Oh! And snoring."

"I don't snore."

"How would you know?"

"I've never heard any complaints." But then again, he never slept over. He did mainly walls, tables, kitchen countertops, fast in-and-out accommodations.

"Snoring is like nose hair. Your dates would never tell you about that either. Only a woman who loved you would tell you something uncomplimentary."

He laughed, then sobered, and then spoke his worst fear. "What if the sex ends us?"

She answered with a confidence only one of them felt. "We won't let it. We'll separate the sex from the rest of our lives."

"How?" he asked miserably.

"I've got it all planned."

"Figures," he said glumly.

"No, seriously, listen! For the next two weeks, we'll only talk about what's happening between us. Block everything and everyone else out. This is about our bodies, not our hearts or heads. Just mindless sex. The hotter the better. I need to be very knowledgeable when I'm with Ted. I don't want anything to give me away as a novice. And then, after the two weeks are up, you'll go on your business trip and I'll start sleeping with Ted. When you return, we'll go on just the same as before, best buds. What could be simpler?"

What they had. That was simpler. And perfect. Now it was gone. Ruined. All because of sex.

Drew hated sex.

Chapter Five

Kesley was sneaking past the second floor on the way to the third when Drew opened his door.

Leaning into the jamb, his shirt unbuttoned and untucked, he grumbled, "What the hell happened to you?"

"You know the saying, 'Stop and smell the roses?' Well, forgetting why I never do, I did. As I was sneezing, I fell into the bush."

"You and your allergies. Get your fanny in here."

"I'm fine," she said, picking a thorn from her knee.

"Get in here, Kes. Those scratches look nasty."

Conscious that their landlady, Mrs. Harris, had her first-floor door cracked and was listening to every word of their conversation, Kesley said loud enough to be overheard, "I won't stay long." Then, lowering her voice, whispered, "My visit has been duly noted by you-know-who."

Drew stepped further out into the hall. "Yooou-hooo, Mrs. Harris." He waved down into the moldy dark stairwell. "I see you, Mrs. Harris."

"Stop that!" Taking his arm, Kesley pulled Drew back from the banister, to where Mrs. Harris could still listen if they spoke loud enough—God bless her—but not actually see them. "The woman is eighty, Drew," she chided. "Nosy is the only fun she gets out of life."

"Hey, I'm all for fun. I say we crank it up. Give her something funner to stick her nose into."

Thus said, Drew picked her up in his arms and carried her back to the banister. Where Mrs. Harris could easily view them, he pulled her into a phony romantic clinch, then proceeded to fake kiss her, his lips making loud smoochie noises.

Not a complete zilch in the dating department, Kes had been kissed *plenty* of times. Drew had kissed her plenty of times too. But she would classify none of her prior kisses as sexual. This wasn't sexual either. Not in the beginning. But then Drew must have forgotten who she was because his formerly closed lips opened and his tongue filled her mouth and the pretend kiss for Mrs. Harris' benefit turned scorching.

So, this is how Drew kisses all his women, Kesley mused, a little taken aback by the hungry sexuality of the kiss, his tongue moving and exploring, his mouth practically eating her, practically devouring her there against the second-floor banister.

"Christ," he said hoarsely, after tearing his lips from hers. "Sorry, sweetheart. I didn't mean for it to go that far."

"Well, *that* certainly made our landlady's day."

Her day too, she thought, letting her head loll against his chest as he carried her inside the apartment and closed the door after them.

Drew's place wasn't dirty, considering a single man lived there alone, but it was devoid of personality. Basically, the three-bedroom flat was utilitarian. Uncluttered. Masculine. Especially the kitchen. Of all the rooms in a home, the kitchen was the domain of the woman. The absence of a feminine touch in Drew's kitchen showed. They ate most of their meals together at her place, but if she moved out she could well imagine him standing up over the stove to eat out of a pot. Or worse yet, not eat in the kitchen at all, choosing instead to eat his meal on a tray in front of the TV. Cheerless image.

Drew perched her on his kitchen counter, like a bird. Like a parrot. Settled between an open jar of peanut butter and its plastic lid, about an inch or so removed from a jelly-sticky knife, she stared down into the sink, where a bowl awaited washing. A lonely spoon straddled the bowl's rim, a few mushy cereal parts clinging.

She sighed. Drew's solitary bachelor's breakfast differed only slightly from the cold slice of morning-after pizza from their college days.

The faded yellow curtains over the sink were clean enough, but ugly, matching nothing else in the room and original to the apartment. One-by-one, his roomies had all moved out, but the faded yellow curtains hung on. Just like Drew and she hung on. Just like cold, day-old pizza, they were leftovers. As far as she could tell, the only remotely new addition was an absurdly ruffled apron folded neatly over the back of a chair, a two-year old gag present she'd given him when the old gang got together to celebrate his birthday. They'd all had a huge laugh over that frilly apron—at the birthday boy's expense. And Drew, laughing at himself along with everyone else, wore that silly apron for the whole night, much to the delight of everyone in attendance. Everyone loved the good-natured Drew.

Kesley craned her neck around the apartment, taking everything in, her eyes resting across the zillion plants she watered when Drew went off on yet another business trip. A traveling consultant keeping plants didn't make sense to her, but keep plants Drew did, all of them flourishing. The man had a wicked green thumb.

Which led her to ask, "Why haven't you moved to a place where you can garden? If not a house, a condo with a backyard. You like growing things."

"A big commitment, sticking something in the ground. Potted plants are portable. They're easy to relocate. I move around a lot."

"What do you mean, you move around a lot? You've lived here a decade, Drew!"

"I didn't know I would be here that long when I moved into the dump."

She let that explanation go, saying, "I would love a house with a yard. I could never afford one on my pay, but dreaming is nice."

"While you're dreaming, pull up your skirt. I want to get a look at your leg."

"I'll do nothing of the sort."

Louisa Trent

"In view of our recent conversations, playing hard to get is kind of ridiculous, don't you think?" Without waiting for an answer, he lunged, pushing her skirt up to mid thigh.

She clamped her hand on top of his. "The deal is we behave as we've always behaved unless we're specifically in sex mode. Are we in sex mode now?"

"No. I'm doing what I would ordinarily do if you fell in a rosebush."

"Okay." She released his hand.

He examined her leg. "Some of these scratches look deep."

Who bothers with pantyhose in the sweltering heat of a city summer? Drew touched *bare* skin as he followed an ugly scratch up along her tanned leg, his finger moving under her skirt as far as her plain, white cotton panties.

With a grunt, he stopped his examination to pull a clean cloth from a drawer and wet it under the tap. "The underwear goes."

Her mouth gaped. "Are you telling me to remove my panties?"

"Yeah. Take 'em off."

"Well, I never!" she gasped in outraged modesty.

"Last night, your tee shirt was nearly around your neck. We both survived. And we both know how far up that scratch goes, and we both know it needs to be cleaned. Get naked."

"No, you get naked," she said in a huff.

"I'm not the one with the thorns."

Too true.

"Drew, last night was different," she still argued. "That was accidental nudity. This is deliberate nudity."

"I don't mean to be crass, but in case you've forgotten, if I do what you asked me to do, I'll be seeing you totally naked soon enough. We'll just consider this a sneak preview. Now don't go all silly on me, sweetheart. It's just you and me here. Two of us in a messy kitchen."

So, he thought she was silly, a silly virgin, did he? Was that how her hesitancy looked to him?

-44-

Well, he was right! Perched on a sink and riddled with thorns was not quite how she had envisioned this moment. What woman wants the first time a man demands the removal of her panties to be the result of a fall into a rosebush?

Too undignified. And washing the scratches wouldn't be enough. Knowing Drew, he'd insist upon painting them with antiseptic. If he had suggested painting her with chocolate he would later lick clean, they'd have themselves a deal, but antiseptic? Un-un. Antiseptic was neither romantic nor erotic.

But, since they weren't in sex mode...

Struggling for composure, Kesley reached up under her skirts.

"Need help?" Drew asked, elbows propped next to her on the counter, chin in hand, tongue hanging out like a lounge lizard on the make for juicy barflies.

She chuckled. "Look, I think I know what you're trying to do and I appreciate the effort. But joking aside, this doesn't come easily for me." In consternation, she bumbled around, not knowing how to proceed. "I'm not used to...you know...undressing in front of a man. I never have before. And this is clinical, not lust-provoked nudity," she squeaked, rubbing her nose with the back of her hand.

"What if I told you this is lust-provoked. Would that help?"

What a dear! To save her dignity, Drew would even lie.

"Not necessary," she relented. "I'm making a complete fool out of myself. Here, I've asked you to have sex with me and I can't even take the first step. Talk about sending mixed messages, huh?"

"You're not doing that, Kes," he said stoutly. So like Drew to boost up her confidence level. "You're no cock-tease."

She plucked at the hem of her skirt. "This is my problem, and I'll just have to deal with it."

"You've got no problem, sweetheart. The situation is the problem. You want real sexual experience, but you're going about it in an artificial way."

"You think I should explain the situation to Ted, and let him be the one—"

"No, no. That's not what I meant." Drew's spine jacked upright. "I just want you to understand what you're letting yourself in for with me. We've known each other ten years, we have something good going on between us and now we're changing the rules."

"Only temporarily, Drew. We'll go right back to the way we were after the two weeks are up."

His usually startling blue eyes suddenly turned remote. "Why don't I give you some privacy?" He handed over the cloth. "I need to get something anyway."

The damn antiseptic. She knew it!

Drew would give her the shirt off his back, but not if the removal of that shirt was a precursor of sex. Having sex with her was an enormous favor, a huge imposition, and she would never have asked it of him if not for the humiliating fact that he was the only man she *could* ask, the only man she had interviewed for the job. But regardless of their closeness, Drew couldn't possibly understand how important this was to her, how desperate was her need for a meaningful personal relationship. Sharing her life with someone, to be part of someone's thoughts in a genuine and significant way, meant everything to her.

She knew how Drew felt about sharing his life with someone, knew his thoughts on intimacy. He wanted no part of either. He had never, not in all the years she'd known him, been serious enough about a woman to bring her back to his apartment. As far as she knew, she was the only woman ever to enter his personal space.

Yanking off her panties, Kesley hid them under her skirt where Drew wouldn't see them—she wasn't at that place yet where she could comfortably leave her underwear out in the open—and then proceeded to wash the dirt and congealed blood around the scratches.

She was tidying up when Drew called from the doorway, "I've got what we need. Can I come back inside?"

"Yes. But everything looks fine, so don't bother playing doctor," she said, grinning nervously up at him as he came to a stand directly in front of her at the counter.

"I'll take a look anyway, if you don't mind. You may have missed some thorns. They're tiny but get infected real easy." Nose to her scratched knee, his fingers gently felt their way over the abrasion.

Kesley grabbed hold of the counter, both hands clasping the rounded edge. "Drew—I was wondering—what kind of ladies' underwear do you like?"

He glanced up. "If you're asking me to cross-dress, I really think we should cover the basics first before moving onto the kink. Mind you, I have no objections to costumes. I've dressed up in all the usual clichés. Cowboy chaps. Gladiator armor. Military SEALs are big right now. Then there was the time the lady insisted I—"

He shook his head. "We won't discuss that particular costume now. Enough to say, it involved a bull whip and animal hide and my screaming in agony."

"You dip." She chortled. "That's not what I meant and you know it! What kinds of lingerie do you prefer your *women* to wear?"

Drew did one of those long exhales he always did when he didn't want to answer a question, and then said, "None."

"No preference? That's not very helpful for when I go shopping. Couldn't you just narrow the field? Color, fabric, style, anything?"

"None."

"You must prefer some over others."

"Kes, sweetheart, I prefer my women without panties. None. Bare-assed."

"Bare-assed. Hmm. Not much of a shopping challenge there. I can do that, I suppose. Bra?"

His eyes went to her breasts. "No bra."

"Clothing? And please don't say, 'None'. I do not want to get arrested for indecency."

"Nude in bed. Dresses in public. No jeans, shorts, or anything with an inseam. Crotchless makes it easier."

"'It' being sex?"

"Usually, but not with you."

"We're not having sex?"

"Nope, we're doing the other thing."

"Fucking?"

"Sweetheart, I have no intention of fucking you. Not ever."

"Now, I'm confused. What other thing?"

"If we're doing this, we're doing it right. I plan on making love to you, Kes."

She waited for the punch line.

There was none.

No humor registered on Drew's face as he smoothed a hand up her thigh under her dress. "I don't feel any thorns."

"Told you!"

Still, he twisted the top off the tube he had in his hand, and placed a small dab on a finger. She was surprised how good the antiseptic smelled, really pleasant.

"Lift your skirt now, sweetheart."

"There are no scratches up that high. I looked."

"We're in sex mode now, Kes."

Her brows rose. "Oh?"

This is not how she thought it would be. She thought they'd be either in his bed or hers, the lights would be off, the shades would be down, and they'd both be naked under the covers. Instead, she was seated on a kitchen countertop in a bright sunlit kitchen, naked from the waist down under her dress while Drew's only concession to nudity was rolled-up shirtsleeves.

He looked up at her meaningfully. "There's no point waiting. We've only got two weeks."

Anxiety attack! Major panic!

"No point waiting at all," she said breathlessly. "I just don't want to rush you. If you have something else you'd rather do—"

"You mean, rather than making love to you?"

"I didn't mean to be coy. It's just that…I know you're busy."

"I cleared my schedule." He pressed his lips to the wispy bangs on her forehead.

Nervous or not, she wanted to savor every moment. Loss of virginity was a one-time only event. In light of that, not wanting to miss anything, she didn't close her eyes as her throat arched and her breasts turned hard and achy. This was what she wanted. This was what she had yearned for. "I trust you with my body, Drew," she whispered.

"No. You honor me with your body."

She gazed up into his face to see if he were serious.

One look into his steadily darkening eyes told her he was absolutely serious. The irreverent Drew was deadly reverent. So unlike him.

"You're such a fucking baby," he said, suddenly sounding angry. "Such a fucking innocent. After this, the boundaries between us will collapse. I'll learn everything about you, and you'll learn everything about me. For two weeks, we'll own each other, body and soul."

"That's not true," Kesley replied, angry now too and not exactly understanding why. "There must be a million people in any given night who have sex without learning a thing about the other person. You're a prime example."

He shook his head. "Not us. Our coming together will be about more than two separate bodies slamming away on a mattress seeking their own separate pleasures. We'll fall in love with each other—it can't be helped. And our lovemaking won't be sterile. Are you prepared for the consequences of that, of the havoc it will create between us?"

Her heart raced. No, it wasn't so! Nothing essential would change between them. There would be no havoc! As Drew always liked to tell her, they got on well together. They were friends, she supposed, though she had never thought about him that way either, because friendship seemed so trite. He was Drew, the man she almost lived with, but without the sex. No matter how horrible her day had been at work, he was the man who made her laugh until she peed her panties. Why wouldn't *that* continue?

It would continue! This would just be a fun interlude, a brief departure from their usual same-old-same-old routine. The comical, never serious Drew, understood fun.

"I'll be your love slave," she said, trying to recapture that spirit of fun. "Your concubine. Your harem woman. I'll ravish you with my body, dance for you naked, peel grapes for you, and then pop them into your mouth, one at a time. For the next two weeks, I am yours totally. Anywhere. Anytime, day or night. Is that prepared enough for you, or do you need it in writing?"

Drew gave her a sad smile. Slowly lowering his jaw to her scratched thigh, he fleetingly touched the bruised area with his lips.

Her sensitized nerve endings immediately reacted. A jolt awakened her womanhood. So close, so close, his lips were so close to the center of her body. She felt like screaming, felt like pulling his head to her vagina so she could melt into the heat of his mouth.

Her grip on the countertop went from relaxed to white-knuckle tight and she moaned.

Drew lifted his jaw. "Now tell me this won't change us."

Dear Lord, he was right! She was changing already. *They* were changing already. She'd been asleep before and now she was awakening. And Drew had felt it.

"That's what I'm talking about, sweetheart," he said quietly, noting her expression. "That's how good it will be with us. That's how hot I'll make you feel. By the time I'm done with you, there won't be an inch of your body I haven't had my mouth on. Now, I'll ask you again before we get in too deep here. Are you prepared to open yourself up to me like that?"

She still felt the spot on her thigh where his lips had all too briefly warmed. The loss of his mouth was almost unbearable. After their two weeks of sex, how would she ever let him go?

She would have to. Drew wasn't interested in marriage, in children. He wasn't even interested in living with her platonically.

How stupid could she get? How had she not understood that sexual magnetism would pulsate between them? How had she thought to fan the flame and not get singed?

Drew knew.

Had he always known? Is that what his comic routine with her was about, a way to keep things superficial, to keep man/woman feelings well within certain safe perimeters?

Drew wasn't immune to her either and his feelings scared him. Now she was scared too. What had she done to them?

Because she craved more, deliberately, with malice of forethought, she had blown apart the safe little asexual cocoon they had shared. By her willful manipulation, she had catapulted them both into a whirlwind of mutual discovery. As a result, would she destroy the connection they had always enjoyed?

"Kes?" he asked insistently.

She remained resolute. Comfort rarely precipitates change, but discomfort always does in some fashion. This was about moving forward. She wanted change! "I'm prepared."

"I hope you are prepared. I hope we both are. Because I have this sinking feeling in my gut that nothing will be the same between us again."

"What are you saying?"

"I'm saying, I'd do anything for you. Anything at all, including this. But I want you to know if I lose you because of this, I'll never forgive you."

Chapter Six

Sometimes it really pissed Drew off the way Kes refused to see the dark lining lurking behind every rainbow. Take them, for instance. She thought the break in their routine would last for only two weeks and then things would return to pre-sex normalcy. That they would go on, the same as before, no change whatsoever.

Ha!

Today was only the first of many steps she would take away from him. That she was taking that first step with him, that he would become physically closer to Kes than ever before, didn't lessen the consequences of what they began here today.

What a dummy, he thought, mentally smacking the heel of his hand against his forehead. Why the hell hadn't the reason behind her discontentment occurred to him before? Kes didn't really want to change her feathers. She just needed a change of nest.

Drew made a swift decision. "I'll start looking for a new place on Monday."

She blinked. "P-pardon? What are you talking about?"

He should have taken this action sooner. Something had been bothering Kes for a while. She'd been discontented. Listless. Smiling less and less. Laughing hardly at all. Sometimes, even his most corny jokes hadn't done the trick. Yeah, he complained about her sunny disposition, her Pollyanna outlook on life, but lately she'd been less cheery than usual and he had missed her bubbly laughter. The way she used to crack up at the lamest stuff. He'd do anything to make her happy. Anything to cheer her up. She didn't like where they lived so he'd fix it. Simple.

He explained. "You're right, this building is a dump. We can do better, we deserve better How's this? We can move into another building, maybe right next door to each other. For sure, on the same floor."

"It's not just the apartment." Kes squinched up her mouth the way she always did when she was perturbed, usually at him. "You're avoiding the issue. I need a man."

Kes was a warm flesh-and-blood woman. Naturally, she had urges. Naturally, she needed a man. Just not Ted. Christ, the guy was a loser. Newly divorced, he was on the make. Prowling for a quick a lay. Anybody would do for Ted.

But Kes was not just anybody.

His sweetheart had stars hanging in her eyes. When she laughed, she lit up like the sky over the Boston Esplanade during the Fourth of July fireworks celebration. He was talking the grand finale, not just the beginning sizzlers. She had a big and beautiful and welcoming heart too. Ted wouldn't appreciate that heart. The jerk would take her goodness for granted. "Okay. Okay. I understand. You need a man. But I'm still looking for a new place."

"Drew, don't get me wrong. I've been happy here. And once it was enough, but we're not in college anymore."

Giving her only half an ear, he kept talking. "I could get a car too. That way, we can widen our search. Look in the 'burbs, too, for a place. Commute to town, Monday through Friday, like everybody else. Hey, it works for me."

"I like living in the city! But get a car, if that's what you want. Me—I want sex. Marriage. A family. The whole deal."

Ted. She had her sights set on Ted. But how could that so-n-so be her whole deal?

Drew felt like he'd been punched in the gut. The prospect of losing Kes hit hard. That he was playing a major part in what would eventually take her away from him just about killed him. He didn't need this kind of irony.

And it wasn't the sex angle. He could handle having another guy's hands on Kes, another guy's dick inside her, as long as it wasn't Ted's hands and dick. If some other guy slept with her, he'd even be man-to-man cordial with the dude if they met on the stairway the next day. Say, the guy—whoever he was, as long as he wasn't that creep Ted—moved in? Drew wouldn't like the arrangement, but he'd learn to live with the deal—

Whoa there! Hold on.

What was he thinking?

Kes wasn't the kind of woman a man lived with. Kes was the kind of woman a man married so she wouldn't get away. What guy in his right mind would drag his feet and risk losing her?

No man on this planet.

She was the kind of woman a guy popped the question to. Once that happened, Drew would lose touch with Kes. Married women never continue close bonds with single male—

Single male *what?* Friends? Is that what they were—friends?

What he felt for Kes went deeper than friendship. Much deeper. She was his whole world. He loved her. Purely. Like a saint. Like a Madonna. Not the singer. The other one.

What the hell? He was coming up with some kind of weird stuff here, really creeping himself out with this sentimental stuff.

Time to lighten the mood. Time for a joke. He'd bring on the heavy artillery. Kes liked his impersonations the best. Especially Bart Simpson. But this called for something original. Something he'd never done before.

Like the best of lecherous pirates, he crooned oily and low, "Separate your legs, me pretty, so I can get at yer precious jewel."

Twittering, Kes separated her thighs. "Please, sir, take the jewel but spare me my life."

The joke sounded unnatural and forced to Drew's ears, and they had never been either with one another. The false note creeping in between them just about wrecked him.

Forgetting himself, he lowered his jaw to claim her lips in a kiss more forceful than he intended, his mouth on her mouth rough, and yeah, angry. Why couldn't she just fuck around like everyone else and forget about Ted?

Slanting his jaw, Drew smashed her lips under his.

Random sex didn't mean anything, and he should know. But so long as she didn't screw up what they had going, he wouldn't mind. He'd give her some experience like he promised, get her up to speed, give her a taste of how good it could be, and then let her loose on the male population. Too busy sowing her wild oats, she wouldn't bother with Ted. It was a plan.

Reaching up her leg, his tongue in her mouth halfway down her throat, he tunneled his hand under her skirt. A smooth move, done so she wouldn't have to bare anything. The consideration was for his sake, not for hers, because, hey, who knew what he would do if he actually saw her area up close? Probably go berserk and turn into a wild animal or something.

The kiss deepening, anger turning back to lust, Drew zeroed in on the pubic curls.

After first refusing to think about that part of her body, he was scoping her now. Strange to touch her there, not exactly incestuous, but forbidden all the same, like he should have his hand cut off or something for daring to cross the line.

God, her fur felt so soft. Like mink under his fingertips. He could've petted her for hours, rubbed his face back and forth and into her pelt.

No more two-day beard growth for him! He wouldn't risk scratching her delicate skin with bristle.

Already, his life had changed—never before had he worried about giving a sex partner whisker burns.

When he found and fingered her heated core, the kiss turned fierce. No finesse. Actually, pretty sloppy, not at all like he normally kissed, which was an art form if he did say so himself. While he sucked hungrily on her mouth, bruising her lips, his tongue taunting her gag reflex, he did the unthinkable— with his lubed middle finger, he separated the folds, and Jesus have mercy, pushed up into Kes.

When she made a little cry into his mouth, he wanted to cry too. The cherry blocked his way, all snuggly tight in place, designed to keep fornicating-prone guys like him out until the wedding night. He had hoped for a technical virginity. That, without her knowledge, she had lost that telling scrap of membrane, maybe bike riding as a kid. If Kes had told him once, she had told him a hundred times, she'd been a tomboy growing up, climbing trees, getting into all kinds of rough-housing mischief. But no, just his kind of bad luck, Kes was a virgin in every sense of the word.

Groaning, he broke the kiss. His forehead grinding to hers, his finger still lodged inside her, all pretense of humor fading away, Drew fought to catch his breath.

This was big. Not just big. B-I-G! Monumental. What did a man say to a woman at a time like this? Upon discovering a female, whom he respected more than he respected himself, had never before been touched, what was he supposed to say? What did he say to Kes, who he had always admired, and who had waited for the right man to come along to do what he was doing now?

Moved by the trust she'd placed in him, he told her the truth. "Nothing's ever been so precious to me."

She hiccoughed a giggle. "What about your comic book collection?"

He rubbed his jaw alongside her nose, his heart racing, his big hand housed between her shapely thighs, his index finger perusing her hymen. "Not even close," he said hoarsely. "Nothing comes close to this. I've never been with your kind before. I avoid your ilk. It's fun and games. It's hooking up, it's fucking around, it's nooners, quickies, sixty-nines, one-night stands…it's not about blood spots on sheets. And I can't do this on a countertop."

But his finger stayed put, right where it was, inside Kes. Even if an earthquake hit, he could not have withdrawn. Nothing in his life had ever felt so right before.

Moisture popped on his forehead, sweat rolled down his back. Like he had stumbled into a sauna wearing all his clothes, never had he felt so uncool. "Before I let you get down, I gotta see it. Please, sweetheart, let me?"

She rolled her eyes. "Men are such visual creatures—"

"I'm serious. Pull the dress up." He could be dominant when the situation required it, and Kes, for all her wanting to shake things up, was glossing over certain basic requirements of sex. Like giving a guy a peek.

Shimmying her hips, she rucked the skirt up around her waist. "The counter feels cold under my ass."

Kes had an ass. Not a rear end. Not a butt. Not even a bottom. A genuine ass. And he was getting a piece of it.

Holy Shit! What a revolting thing to think about a saint Only, he was allowed to think those kinds of guy thoughts now, seeing she had opened things up.

He wanted more things opened up, because the glimpse she was allowing him was not nearly enough. He was thinking IMAX, like a wide-screen presentation at the Omni Theatre at the Museum of Science.

Drew swallowed. Hard. "Kick off the sandals, put your feet up on the counter."

Afraid of missing something, he didn't blink while she maneuvered.

He waited—a contortionist wouldn't have had a problem with the pose or someone double-jointed, but Kes was neither.

And he was no caveman, still he managed a good imitation of a Neanderthal grunt. "How come your knees are touching?"

"Because I'm not at the GYN's?" She grinned.

The saucy routine didn't fool him. His sweetheart was a human wreck, and there was nothing he could do to make it any easier for her, except stay matter-of-fact about the whole uneasy business of seeing her up close and personal for the very first time.

He motioned her to open, a modified two-handed spreading signal universally understood.

Feet together on the counter, she widened her knees.

"How ya doin'?" he asked, not looking down. Staring directly into her eyes until his own started watering.

"Fine. Just fine." She looked away.

"No You need to look. Looking is part of it, and not just for the man. Looking excites the woman too. So look."

"I've seen it before, you know. I'm a virgin, not a silly nitwit."

"You're the most intelligent woman I've ever known, Kes. But you've never seen my hand there. So look."

She did glance down then, as his free hand—the fingers none-too-steady—moved along the inside of each of her thighs.

He looked too, at his wrists, wide and sinewy, sparsely covered in wiry light hair, there between her legs. He never thought to see his hand there, his index finger penetrating the pink slit.

So dirty, so raunchy, so transcendental, seeing his hand covering the notch.

"You have such soft skin. Lovely, dewy skin," he said, bending so he was eye level to the good stuff. "So sweet here."

"The opening night, the grand unveiling." She gulped. "You're the first man ever to see me," she said, answering the question going around in his lurid/sacred thoughts.

"Oh, yeah?" They'd never gone there before, never even broached the subject, but she held his rapt attention now. "No petting?"

"Some above the waist, over-the-clothing petting. You know, in high school. But nothing more. In college, my refusal to jump into bed the first time out with a man ended any subsequent dates. It was an issue of time. I needed it. And no one wanted to invest it to get to know me first. So, here I am, a one-date wonder."

What those stupid, impatient, sex-jocks had missed, Drew mused, blowing a humid breath across the sensitive region of her...of her...

He didn't have to say it aloud, but he did have to think it. Unnatural not to think it. Every guy thought it. When a man got this close, pussy automatically got upgraded.

To cunt.

He was blowing a moist breath of air across his sweetheart's cunt.

Kes held herself steady, but Drew wondered if inside she shivered and trembled and quivered, like he shivered and trembled and quivered.

"Will you be a screamer?" he asked. "Now that you've given me permission to start wondering, I have all these questions. It will take me a while to get readjusted to thinking them. Do you understand? I can't rush this. It's too important. But don't worry—we'll fit it all in. Everything you want to do."

Lowering his head again, Drew blew another breath across her pretty cunt, so sweet and sexy under the fragile eyelet lace of her slip, a feminine undergarment that still covered much of her upper thighs. Smiling his delight, he watched the weightless lace dance for him, as he hoped Kes danced for him in her thoughts, as he danced for her in his.

Not a fast dance.

A slow dance.

Just for Kes.

Chapter Seven

A fragrant small envelope waited for Kesley inside her mailbox at work. A stamp-free upper right-hand corner confirmed someone had hand-delivered the message.

Heart pounding, she opened the flap.

The folds of the scented yellow stationary contained a masculine scrawl.

Kes, sweetheart—meet me at Gordon's Furniture after work. Consider this is a rendezvous. Drew

Not having seen nor heard from Drew since her fall into the rose bushes, she thought he had decided to renege on his promise. Thought he had set out to deliberately avoid her. Horrible to admit, but the note set her mind at ease.

Kesley hugged the envelope to her chest.

She should have known better, should have had more faith in Drew. He always kept his word. Rather than skip town without telling her, he had initiated a rendezvous. Imagine that! A secret assignation. How incredibly sweet and romantic of him.

Drew had written her notes before. Messages jotted on the back of a shopping bag or scribbled on a sticky note and stuck on her kitchen table. The most elaborate letter involved picking up a carton of moo-shi pork on the way home from work. *That* he had hastily written on a sheet torn from a legal-sized note pad. Now this A message on rose-scented stationary. The uncharacteristic gesture pulled at her heartstrings.

"Anything wrong, Kesley?" Doris looked up from the fax machine to ask. "That was a mighty big sigh."

Snapping out of her reverie, Kesley turned to the fellow social worker. "I sighed?"

Doris gave a worried nod. "Still concerned about John Smith?"

"No, actually I'm feeling better about him today. He kept the dental appointment I made for him with the Mobile Med Van, so things are looking up. But I'll still hit the streets with you and the outreach team. You know, do a follow-up, see how it went with the health screening."

"You know our schedule, every weekday night 2 to 10, we make the rounds."

She nodded. "I'm there."

Though not an official member of the outreach street-worker team Kesley still, upon occasion, canvassed the spots where homeless kids hung, primarily to touch base with youths at high risk. Sometimes just talking, showing a troubled teen someone cared, that *you* cared, could diffuse a crisis.

John Smith—phony name, phony age, belligerence not remotely phony—was a crisis in the making. Unlike many of the four-hundred plus runaways and adolescents The Shelter serviced every year, this kid had potential. He could straighten out, rejoin the mainstream…make it. But he tottered on the edge, could go either way—drop out for good or find a way back into productive society.

In his case, because he was young, family intervention and mediation might work. Before broaching the subject of reconciliation, she had to gain his trust. Trust took time to earn, and her time with him was a dwindling commodity. After years of working with kids, she knew that edgy, ready-to-run look street kids wore. For some reason, John Smith had hit the wall. To reach him, she would need to work fast. Then, if the Band-Aid approach worked and John stayed in town, she could slow it down. These kids carried deep scars. No quick and simple fix worked. For long-standing and complicated problems like theirs, offering support, but not pushing, spelled the key to success.

If—and in this business, *if* was one gigantic two-letter word—they developed a relationship, maybe then she could prompt John Smith to drop a dime and call home. If the situation there was unsalvageable, if the factors that caused him to leave home were horrendous, returning to his family might not be the optimal or even a possible option. If John Smith couldn't reconcile with his family, if reunification wasn't in the cards, then she would work towards arranging an alternate living situation for him.

IF. IF. IF.

No IF in empowerment. Making a kid part of the decision-making process, directing a runaway in such a way that he would want to take responsibility for his own life, always produced a positive consequence.

John Smith had taken that first step—he had kept his medical appointment. That offered her encouragement. Fairly sure he worked as a male prostitute, Kesley needed to get him tested for HIV and STDs, and a myriad of other medical and psych services.

Ordinarily, she would have used Drew as a sounding board. While blowing off psycho-babble with a snort and some adolescent potty language, he instinctively seemed to understand the nitty-gritty reality of how teenage boys got by on the streets, how they thought, where they congregated.

Drew had a real empathy for homeless kids. He even employed a few "success stories" in his business. And there *were* success stories. Some kids got with the program and availed themselves of the supportive opportunities.

Kesley would like to have shared her concerns about John Smith with Drew, but for these two weeks, she had decided against talking shop with him. She would probably burst at the seams holding it all in, but she really did need to recharge the batteries, grab some time for herself. If she didn't take a break from the job, the job might break her.

Burnout happened all the time in human services. Having a life outside the job went a long way towards prevention. She'd put a personal life off for far too long.

Not anymore. Time for a change. Time to grab a little happiness. Time to find a guy and make things happen. Way past time to start having sex. What had held her back?

Only herself.

When she looked in the mirror, she saw a plain woman staring back. Nothing about her generic features would ever catch anyone's attention, particularly a man's attention. And that was okay, because sometimes, a nondescript appearance served as a helpful tool—

No one ever saw her as a threat. Basically, people overlooked her. Who noticed a little brown mouse?

In regards to her kids, the little brown mouse roared like a lion.

As a social worker, she advocated for young people amidst the confusing tangle of bureaucratic red tape, representing those without a voice. Knowing how a nonentity feels, she made sure her kids were both heard and seen. She did it with a vengeance, her vocal cords loud and strong and persistent, her verbal pictures of lost kids as vivid as she could make them. She wore the system down until her teens got what they needed. When the directors of governmental and private agencies saw her coming, they ran and hid—from her, the little brown mouse. And she went right after them. No one escaped her Mighty Mouse advocacy.

If she could only speak up for herself and her own needs as easily.

She would start today. The sun shone like a big yellow beach ball up in the clear blue sky, she was no longer down in the dumps about John Smith, and she had an appointment that didn't involve crisis intervention.

After carefully folding the paper back into the envelope, Kesley placed Drew's rendezvous note in her jacket pocket. The Shelter was an informal place. Unless she had a meeting to attend, she generally dressed casually— jeans and a cotton shirt for the most part. Dressing down made the kids less suspicious of her as an adult authority figure. But since Drew made a point of saying he liked his women in skirts, she had worn a sleeveless floral print dress with a crisp linen jacket to work. Since she had a predominantly male caseload, she never wore anything revealing. After the rendezvous with Drew, she would change into jeans, then hit the streets for outreach. A long day followed by an even longer night.

Squeezed cheek-to-jowl between two busy streets, the antique store was located about a block away from The Shelter. She frequented the shop with such embarrassing regularity, not only did she know the names of the owner's seven kids, but she also knew their birthdays. Excited about the tryst, Kesley raced all the way there.

Mr. Gordon looked up when she entered the showroom. "Need help? Give a holler."

At her nod, the proprietor returned to reading his newspaper.

Since Drew was never early for anything, and rarely even on time, she was shocked to find he'd already arrived for their date. Elegantly slumped against a wing-backed chair, he stiffly lifted his sculpted lips in salute, no trace of his usual easy-going style anywhere in evidence. Though the same bad-boy, devil-may-care crinkles fanned out from the corners of his hooded eyes, this smile was stamped "adult".

She smiled back, equally adult. Not rated X, but a strong R.

Suddenly, he stuck his hands in his pockets, which in turn caused his broad shoulders to hunch. Tufts of thick blond hair fell carelessly over his forehead. He looked just like a little boy caught with his hand in the cookie jar.

Cookie-jar. Uh—that would be her.

No complaints. What woman wouldn't want to be a gorgeous man's forbidden temptation?

She had started having forbidden feelings for Drew too, just as he had warned would happen. By asking for this favor, she had apparently opened up Pandora's Box. Her flesh actually tingled with heightened sexual awareness…

Then again, might be she was having an allergic reaction to all the dusty antiques.

Holding back a sneeze, Kesley waved just like always.

Two striding steps brought Drew to her side. Since the man never hurried, this amazed her.

He leaned down, and whispered, "You look beautiful."

She looked the same as always. Okay, maybe a little different because of the dress, but basically the same. Though compliments don't grow on trees, Drew, the flirt, always sprinkled her liberally with praise, so his off-handed remark bounced right off.

"Thanks," she wheezed out.

He scowled. "Did you run here?"

"All the way," she admitted breathlessly. "I was afraid I'd arrive late and you'd leave and I'd die a virgin and..."

"Come here, you." Taking her hand, Drew led her deeper into the store.

Confusion took hold. "Where are you taking me?"

"Downstairs. I need to show you something. Don't argue. Just come."

She grinned. "Coming is the whole point of your agreeing to help me."

He smirked, just like the old Drew. Only different. Then ordered, "Put it in motion."

"Oh goody. I love domineering men. At least I think I do, but lacking in experience, I could be mistaken," she replied as Drew tugged her along downstairs to the basement, where Mr. Gordon kept the best goods. After kicking some dusty boxes out of his way, he stood her before a cheval mirror.

She checked the price. Not bad. If she sold a kidney. On her social worker's salary, she'd have to save up to afford the cobwebs.

"Stop looking at the tag," Drew admonished, "and concentrate on the beauty straight ahead."

"Huh? Where?" Swiveling her neck, she surveyed the area. "I can't see a thing—the friggin' mirror's in the way."

Clamping his hands on her shoulders, he forced her chin up with his index fingers. "Look at your reflection."

No way to really avoid it—she'd only just told him so. "Yeah?"

"Look hard."

Her muscles must've tightened under his grip because he started massaging her neck. "Now listen to me."

In utter abandonment, her head fell back against him and she stared at the ceiling.

"Are you listening to me?"

"Uh-huh."

"You're beautiful. Very beautiful. Any man who gets you is damned lucky."

"Keep talking. I might keep you around."

"Do that. Keep me around. You've kept me around for a decade already." Massaging changed to kneading.

"Mmm." She heaved an orgasmic sigh. At least she *thought* it was orgasmic, but lacking in experience, she didn't know for sure. "Don't stop what you're doing. You're awfully good at this."

"So I've been told."

Probably only by a million or so women...

Kesley sniffed. "Okay, I admit it. I'm like putty in your hands. But you know, eventually, with time, putty gets all dried up. Cracked and crumbled, the putty breaks and then the glass pane it was holding falls out and shatters. That's how I feel inside. Dried-up. Like I'm about to crack. Don't let me break, Drew. Please?"

The massaging came to a stop and a set of knuckles skimmed her cheekbone. "You are the most irritating, exasperating, beautiful woman I've ever known. You're not drying up like a spinster in some damn Victorian novel. I'll walk you through all the first-time sex stuff. Show you some tricks. By the time I'm done, hell, you'll get any guy you want."

"Any guy I want, huh?"

"Yep. You bet. Guaranteed."

"Good. Because I don't want to die a virgin."

He braced her shoulders against his chest. "You won't die a virgin. I made you a promise and I'm keeping it. And when we're done, you'll cut a mile wide swath through all the eligible men in Boston."

Her fluttering lashes tagged his in the glass. "Yippee. Swath-cutting. I can't wait. Let's get started."

Chapter Eight

Another time, Drew might have laughed off his sweetheart's tasteless show of enthusiasm. Not today. For some reason, today he found her eagerness for sexual experience amazingly unfunny.

Meaning to tell her so, he spun her around to face him. But before he could spit out the words, her lush mouth played him for a fool.

Moronic to fight it, when every cell in his body screamed for the connection with the kind of physical urgency that defied good intentions. Why beat himself up over something he couldn't help? Surrendering to an impulse more holy than base, he let desire rule.

And tasted her.

For something that came out of nowhere, that had snuck up on him when he had least expected it, the kiss gained momentum fast. With a snowballing effect, before long, the kiss had a life of its own, an energy of its own, a pulse of its own. A living organism, independent of its creator, the kiss overpowered him like a monster, like Frankenstein, only a hell of a lot nicer.

Drew pulled Kes closer, his mouth opening over hers until their tongues met, coiled, entwined. He gave himself over to the wave of heat, surfing the fire, hoping not to wipe out in the flames as he took the ride of his life.

Kes sure as hell didn't kiss like a virgin.

As the kiss sizzled and popped, her giving mouth going from softly clinging to full-throttle sexual hunger, Drew couldn't tell which of them fueled the fire, and it so didn't matter when she came up for breath and whispered a demanding "More" in his ear.

So much for teaching her lip-locking techniques. Looked to him like they could skip the prerequisites and move right onto advanced subjects...

On second consideration, he just wasn't ready to make the jump from beginner to expert. After all, they'd only known each other ten years.

"How much more?" he asked, hunting down excuses. "You know, we are in the middle of Gordon's. Think of the shoppers. You wouldn't want them to catch an eyeful."

"There's no one here. And who cares anyway?"

That was what he thought she'd say.

He produced another delaying tactic. Lame, but worth a shot. "Take a breath first," he replied, gasping for air himself. "Ya gotta learn how to breathe in between. Otherwise, you can get the bends."

She squinted up at him in that adorable way of hers. "Bends? Only scuba divers get the bends."

"Au contraire. The bends can happen to anyone who doesn't come up for breath. Kissers, in particular, are at risk. Young urban professionals in their mid-twenties have the highest susceptibility factor. You should see the stats." He shuddered. "Horrible. And it's communicable too."

"The numbers don't apply to us," she argued, pulling in a few easy inhales while his own heart hammered and his lungs felt about ready to explode. "We're beyond the age limit."

He gawked at her. Christ, she was right Incredibly, they were too old for his made-up myth. Somewhere along the line, they had both become grownups.

After that brush with his own mortality, Drew lost his edge. Fell out of game. Why were they, two responsible, mature adults, necking like teenagers in the basement of a dirty furniture store? They should go get a room somewhere. Better yet, an apartment somewhere. Best still, some real estate, a house where they could put down roots. Together. They could get a twin set of rockers, install them on the front porch, and when they were both decrepit, creak back and forth while reminiscing about all the good times. Growing old didn't seem scary at all, with Kes rocking by his side—

"More," the tyrant ordered again, booting him right in the fantasy.

He gasped. "I'll see what I can do."

Dipping his jaw, he took the plunge, a voluntary free-fall into Kes.

Naturally, she took full advantage, her palms moving wildly over him, while Drew kept his own hands securely glued to his sweetheart's shoulders.

Going up on her toes, she combed her fingers through his hair, groaned into his mouth, "Oh, Drew, Drew. Kiss me, Drew, kiss me, kiss me, kiss me. Keep on kissing me."

"Kes, sweetheart, we'll end up on the floor if we keep going at it like this."

"I don't care."

"But the floor is all dirty and stuff."

"I don't care."

"But—but your pretty dress will get all ruined."

The little wanton made a wounded noise at the back of her throat, something between a mew and a moan. "I don't care."

Hauling her arms up over his shoulders, Drew hoisted Kes up the length of his body, anchoring his bulge to her sweet hollow. Mindlessly, their bodies grinding together, her yellow dress crushed like flower petals between them, he growled, "This is definitely not a good idea." Half-walking her, half-carrying her, he scraped them along the wall until they hunkered together under the stairwell, where there was some privacy. "This is not a good idea at all."

"I don't care."

"Funny, you're saying that." He kissed her hard, one ear listening for customer footsteps on the tread above them.

She gyrated against his zipper, her sexy undulations making him insane, and he cupped her bottom, only to hold her still. But one palm, somehow, he didn't know how, ended up beneath her skirts and slid over her ass, and found no between-the-cheeks thong. No scrap of silk. Cotton panties. Little-girl innocent panties. The kind that go clear up to the waist. He froze.

"Yes, Drew, yes."

"Un-un. Hell no. No fucking way. I'm good, but I ain't that good. I can't do what you want me to do, not here." Especially not with a woman who wore cotton underwear. And how come, all of a sudden, he found modest briefs sexy as hell?

He pressed his forehead to hers. "Sweetheart, we need to save this vertical stuff for later. We've already skipped the tutorial on kissing, no way am I plowing ahead to the graduation ceremony."

"Pardon?" she chirped, a bird itching to leave the nest way too soon.

If Kes took off now, maybe she'd fly straight over that rainbow she saw all the time. Then again, maybe she'd flop on her beak and get her feathers all mussed.

He wasn't taking chances with her first time. When they did the deed, he wanted perfect. No crushed feathers, no dented beak, over the rainbow all the way. "I said, this position is too advanced for the beginner."

He slid her down his body, and pointed to the stairs above their heads. "Besides, I hear footsteps. Customers. They're headed our way."

When Kes opened her mouth to argue, he put a finger to her lips. "And please don't say, 'I don't care' because I do care. A hell of a lot. I don't want you caught with me like this."

"You're no fun."

"Hey, consider this sexual boot camp. You want fun—wait 'till the end of the damn training. Then, I'll be fun. Right now, you're still a know-nuthin' recruit."

She didn't say a word, not when he put her away from him, not when he bent to straighten her dress. How come Kes wasn't talking?

Drew wiped his sweaty palms on his jeans.

Kes always talked things out, through, and over. A social worker to the core, she would tackle the most sensitive topics. The kind of complicated, not-so-nice stuff most folks wouldn't touch with a ten-foot pole. That stuff most people wanted swept under the carpet, out of sight, out of mind.

Louisa Trent

Not Kes.

She fearlessly shone a hundred-watt bulb into the darkest places. That light bulb explained why she was so good at helping kids in trouble. She not only cared, she was one tough lady. The places she went at night with those street-workers, the situations she encountered day in and day out, the problems of those kids...would break most people's optimism.

Not Kes.

She remained hopeful throughout it all.

"You look so pretty, like a pretty yellow rose. Did I tell you that yet?" he asked.

When she remained quiet, he gently touched the corner of her swollen mouth. "Kes? Aren't we talking today?"

Her silence was more than he could stand.

Drew pulled her close again, pathetically grateful that the footsteps descending the treads prevented another go 'round of heavy petting. With Kes, he wanted to do things right, and doing the wild thing in a stairwell just wasn't right. Not for Kes.

"We'd better leave," he whispered against her soft hair. "You go up first. There's a bed upstairs I want you to see. White canopy on top with a curtain enclosure, solid mahogany, Williamsburg reproduction—you can't miss it"

When she left, Drew scrubbed both palms over his face, and then smashed his clenched fist against the wall. Shit, piss, and corruption How the hell could he go through with this?

He went through the motions with sex. By rote, he'd satisfy whoever he was with first, before getting his too. No complications. No making it out to be more than a good time.

Sex wouldn't be like that with Kes. Sex with her...sex with her...

Making love to Kes would mean something.

Was he ready for meaningful sex?

Drew broke out in a sweat, indecision plaguing him, doubts sinking in.

-72-

Bottom line—he would do anything for Kes. Do anything to make her happy. Even run the risk of messing with his own head. The prospect of making love for the very first time terrified him. And he'd do it anyway. With Kes. *For* Kes.

That kiss. That wet, hungry, cock-hardening kiss. Where had Kes learned to kiss like that?

Balls aching, Drew stumbled up the stairs, still walking funny when he arrived at the top and Kes said conversationally, "Nice bed."

Good. They were talking again. "Ya think?"

"I do. Yes. The bed is not at all what I thought you'd pick."

"I'm glad you like it." He strolled lazily over to join her, the easy gait costing him.

Kes puckered her brow. "But why go to all the expense?"

"Used to be, a man and his bride would begin their married life in a bed like this, their babies would get birthed in a bed like this, they'd die in a bed like this, and then the bed would get passed down to one of their children. A bed like this means something. It has a history. I like that idea."

Drew blew a puff of air on the elegantly carved post, and then, buffed the coin-sized area with his flannel shirt cuff until the spot gleamed. With a satisfied pat, he went on to check the headboard, actually grabbing it with both hands and giving it a shake. When it didn't fall apart, he bent to check the bed's underpinnings.

"Nice," she offered again.

He straightened. "So you really like the bed?"

"I was talking about your butt."

"Shhh. Someone might hear."

"If you didn't want me to admire the scenery you shouldn't have flaunted your flanks at me like that." She tilted her head for a better view of his back pockets.

"I wasn't flaunting my *flanks*. What am I, a hunk of meat on a butcher's hook? A person's self-worth should not be…well…hung on superficiality."

She smirked. "Yeah, well, those snug jeans certainly give your self-worth a boost. And speaking of well hung…"

"Do *not* say it, Kes."

She laughed. "I calls 'em as I sees 'em. And in those jeans, I sees a substantial package."

His looks, his substantial package, had always attracted notice. From both sexes. Frankly, more often than not, the attention was a nuisance. Worse, the attention made him feel like a pretty boy and reminded him of a dark period in his life that he'd just as soon forget. He took no pride in what stared back at him from the shaving mirror. And it really pissed him off that Kes thought maybe he did.

"For your information, Kes, these are the jeans you coerced me into buying when we went shopping two summers back. Today's the first time I've ever worn them. Secondly, I was checking the bedsprings for tension, not shaking my booty. And go light on the character analysis, would you? I'm already riddled with self-doubts."

"Stop it! You've never suffered an insecure moment in your life."

He went back to checking bedsprings. "Shows how little you know me."

"Don't try to convince me you're riddled with feelings of inadequacy because I'm not buying it."

"That's okay—we're here to buy a bed."

She settled herself on the edge of the mattress. "If you buy the bed, does this mean that Operation Deflower is ready to roll?"

He looked over his shoulder. "I need a place to put the bed first. It won't fit in my current bedroom."

She threw herself backwards on the pillows. "The bed fits pretty good here." She patted the space next to her.

"Better get up before a customer sees you."

"No one will see if we close these fancy curtains. See?" She reached for the drawstring and gave a pull. Like magic, the enclosure started to move around the bed.

"Hold on there!"

Kes flung the drawstring aside. "You don't want me vertical. You don't want me horizontal. How do you want me?"

"I want you..." *Period*. He thought.

He shook his head. "Never mind what I want. Just get up."

"Not yet. This bed is so comfy." She kicked off her yellow sandals and flopped backwards again, this time with her hands thrown over her head. "Join me?"

"Not here. The customers..."

"Relax. They're looking for a kitchen table, not bedroom furniture. I overheard their conversation." She wiggled on the coverlet. "By the way, I should tell you on a scale of one-to-ten, you kiss about a nine. I've made out with some of the best and you're right up there with Nick Olsen."

"Nick Olsen? Who the hell is he?" His hands rode his belt loops.

In her prone position, Kes tucked her legs to the side. "Nick played tuba in the NU's band. He was a gifted musician with an outstanding pair of lips." She smiled, sexy as all hell. "But as good as Nick was, I'd have to say that for sheer puckering power, you've got him licked."

He frowned. "You said you had no experience."

"I said I was a virgin, and you can back up that assertion. But I never said I was dateless. Before we met, I went out. Not a lot, but some. I just never went very far, if you get my meaning."

"I get your meaning." His gaze fell to her mouth. "You give pretty good lip service yourself, by the way."

She shrugged. "Thank you, sir. When a girl doesn't go to home plate she learns to make the most of first base."

He cleared his throat. "Didn't any guy try to steal to second?"

"Sure they tried, but I was firm in my resolve to stay put. Most of my dates didn't push. Those who did got a knee in the family jewels. That would explain why I didn't get asked out on second dates," she twittered.

Drew bent over Kes, his outstretched arms bracketing her shoulders. "The bed seems sturdy enough. It should stand up to some major bouncing."

She grinned up at him. "Bouncing, huh? I like the sound of that."

"Good. I'm taking it."

Her head popped up off the pillow. "The bed is really ours?"

Ours—he liked the sound of that.

Retracting his arms, Drew turned to examine a lamp. "Yep, ours. In fact, I've decided to take the whole five-piece set."

With an energetic leap, Kes was up on her feet and adding numbers on the tags. "At these prices, this bed is sure to impress your future ladies."

He ran a finger over the lampshade. "I'm not thinking about impressing the ladies." He was only thinking about impressing Kes. "Remember? This is just about you and me. No work stories, no talking about other people in our lives. Let's be selfish. Agreed?"

Kes nodded. "Agreed. But since you're picking up the cost of the bed, let me take care of the bed linens. What shall I get—black satin?"

"Nope. Plain cotton, the kind married people use." Drew gestured to the lamp he'd been admiring. "Do you think this goes with the bed?"

"It's lovely. But I think you should go with the one over there."

The "one over there" had a red-light district velvet shade with dingly-dangly glass prisms. Around the base, brass ladies did a naked ribbon dance.

Not for him. "I'll stick with the old-fashioned lamp. Why don't we leave the other one for the local bordello?"

"Your bedroom, your call." Kes smoothed her dress. "Uh-oh I forgot. I'm wearing panties. And a bra. You told me no underwear. I'll take 'em off." Bending forward, her hands disappeared under her full yellow skirts.

A pulse hammered in his temple, another pulse drummed lower down. "You can't do that here."

"Oh yeah?"

In the mirror behind her, he glimpsed the pale curve of an exposed buttock. "Do not lift those skirts in the middle of this showroom There are security cameras. Customers. *Reflections*," he hissed.

"But your women don't wear undergarments, you told me so yourself." Her hips started rolling in a distinctively female, panties-descending kind of way.

He clutched his chest. "I'm having a heart attack here."

"Nonsense. You're only thirty."

"*Only* thirty," he whined, playing on her sympathies. "That's almost middle-aged. How many good erections do I have left? You strip naked in this showroom and fear of arrest will render me impotent. Where will your maidenhead be then?"

Her eyes drifted to the bulge in his jeans. "Did you say, impotent?"

"That's left over from when I woke up this morning. Every guy gets one first thing."

"Drew, it's almost 6 p.m."

"What can I say? I overslept."

She angled her head. "Fine. I'll go change behind that ornamental screen in the corner. Feel free to watch. This screen is wonderful," she enthused, disappearing from sight behind it. "I've always wanted one. This won't take long—"

"Can't you do this striptease in the privacy of your own home, as in later, after work?" he groused, going after her.

"What later? After work, I'm working too. Tonight, I'm riding with the outreach team."

Prickles stabbed the back of Drew's neck. Kes only did outreach on the most serious cases, kids she feared losing to the streets.

Knowing a lost kid always broke her heart, Drew sidled up to the screen. "Wanna talk about it?"

"For two weeks, we're not talking about work, just sex. Remember?"

Yeah, he remembered. But they didn't live in a vacuum, and he could tell Kes needed to talk. "We can make an exception, just this one time. C'mon," he wheedled. "Tell me what's going on."

"Nope. We both need a break from outside interference."

"Outside interference? That's called life. No one can take a break from life."

"Drew—do edible panties count as underwear?"

"W-what?" he stammered, her lightening-quick change of subject throwing him a curve.

"Edible panties. What flavors do you like? What about peppermint?"

"Kes, why don't we talk—?"

White cotton briefs skidded out from behind the screen, a white cotton bra and a white nylon slip followed. Then out popped a face bearing a pair of laughing eyes. "Oops"

"Don't you *oops* me. You did that on purpose."

On a run, Drew scooped up the undies, and jammed them in his pockets. Giving her a killer look, he walked back to the screen. "You done?"

"I'm stark naked. Wanna peep?"

"Certain things should be saved for a private moment. Stark nakedness is one of them," he said primly, refusing to look, but wanting to look, wanting to do more than look. He wanted to do unspeakable things to Kes behind that decorative screen. One involved his palm and her rosy bottom.

Timing was everything when a man sets the stage for lovemaking and everything had to be right.

He was not right. Not edgy like this, not lusty like this. For Kes, he wanted respectful and respectable. Neither described the middle of a furniture store.

"Here I am," Kes finally said, stepping out from behind the screen.

Even if his pockets weren't filled to capacity with feminine unmentionables, Drew would've known she wore nothing under that summer dress, would've known only a thin layer of sunny yellow fabric covered bare-naked woman, because two clues of her unfettered state pointed right at him.

Tempted to reach out and thumb those two clues, Drew took a giant step backwards. "I should...you know...pay up at the register."

"And I should get back to work." She held out a hand. "My underwear?"

From the safety of distance, he gave them a toss. "Kes, I think we should talk about your doing outreach tonight with the street-workers. How serious is this case? Can I do anything to help?"

"Thanks for offering, but everything is under control. Not to worry."

What the hell did she think? Did she think if she said the words, just like that, like damn magic, the worry disappeared? She had just slammed a door in his face, and he was just supposed to smile and accept it?

Kes had never done that to him before, had never shut him out of her life, and he wasn't about to take it without fighting back. "People who have sex still talk, Kes."

"Have you ever had a serious discussion with any of your sexual partners?"

He snorted.

Reflex. Her round, jiggling breasts had him coming and going. He wasn't thinking straight.

"See?" she said triumphantly.

"But you and I have always talked."

"I talk, you listen. You joke, you tease, you cheer me up. You tell me funny made-up stories. I don't know anything about your life before you moved downstairs from me. I've never met your parents, while my folks have practically adopted you."

"I love your parents, Kes. They've got great taste in adopted sons."

She narrowed her eyes at him. "Do not expect me to cry on your shoulder any more."

Yeah, now she had Ted's shoulder to cry on. The prick.

Kes checked her watch. "Gotta run," she said, and did.

Drew didn't know what he'd done, what he'd said, but he could feel his sweetheart's anger simmering just below the surface. What the hell did she want from him? He was doing everything she asked. What more did she expect him to do?

Funked-out, pissed off too, he slumped his way to the register.

After squaring away the bedroom set and lamp, Ralph Gordon fingered his glasses up along the narrow bridge of his nose. "Will that be all, sir?"

"Nope. I'll take the screen with the blue peacock too."

"The lady's changing screen?" the storekeeper asked all smarmy-like

"That's the one."

"Gift for your maiden aunty?"

Drew leaned an elbow on the counter. "Nope. The screen is for me. I'm the modest type." He fluttered his lashes.

Gordon yawned, handed over the receipt. "Funny man."

Once maybe. Not any more. Drew had definitely lost his touch.

Why was he doing this? he wondered, leaving the store and heading back to the apartment. Why had he ever agreed? They had a perfect thing going. What was he doing screwing with perfect?

Chapter Nine

Once, Kesley could spot a street kid a block away. But after driving around the inner-city parks and neighborhoods in the outreach van for half the night, canvassing the usual hangouts for John Smith, all the kids looked street to her.

"I don't see him," she said, squinting out the front passenger window.

"Okay. I'll drive through the Fenway." Harvey Gold made a fast U-turn.

They chugged down a narrow side-street dotted with clubs on both sides. A rock show must have just let out, because kids were spilling out onto the sidewalks.

Nose pressed to the glass, Kes spotted a group of teens. The kids, about twenty in all, of every shape and color and hairstyle, loitered outside a convenience store. At least three of the faces seemed familiar to her.

She turned to the van driver. "Let me out here."

Doris, used to doing nightly outreach, leaned forward from the back seat. "You think you see him?"

"Yeah. That's him. John Smith is the tall slender one in the middle of the crowd. The one in the long-sleeve wool shirt, tight jeans, carrying a leather jacket with patches."

Doris shook her head. "Long sleeves in the summer—is he a heroin addict?"

Kesley blew a breath up into her limp bangs. "My gut tells me no. I just don't think he's in that deep yet."

The van pulled over to the side, and she hopped out.

Harv stuck his head out the window after her. "Want me to buddy-up with you?"

"I'm okay. John is belligerent and scared, not a threat."

"All right. We won't crowd you. I'll park the van behind that drug store across the street and wait for you, out of sight."

In the dark, wearing jeans and sneakers and no make-up, Kesley could still pass for a young adult. This worked in her favor during outreach. Cramp a kid's style in front of his peers, and you lost the kid.

Hands in her pockets, she ambled on over to the congregation, side-stepping to John. "Hey."

Bloodshot eyes widened at her. John Smith gave no other outward indication that he knew her. "Yeah, hey."

"Think we can talk?" She motioned to the side. "In private."

"Sure."

"She your bitch?" hooted a young lady with a purple and red hairdo.

Another boy hollered, "Snap! Watch out."

After giving the obligatory finger salute to his hecklers, John led the way through a broken chain link fence, rounding on her alongside a blue dumpster. "What the fuck are you doing here, Miss Richmond?"

No use trying to snow him, she told him the truth straight-up. "Looking for you."

"Why?"

"Part of The Shelter's service, John."

"Even doctors don't make house calls no more."

She looked around. "This where you crash?"

"Yeah. Welcome to my digs. Care to take a seat?" He gestured to a black garbage bag plumped like a pillow. A city rat scooted over a broken beer bottle.

Kesley shook her head. "I'll stand, thank you."

John raised a brow. "Wanna see my new stud?"

"Sure thing."

He stuck out his tongue—she hadn't been expecting that—and gold gleamed in the moonlight. "The old dudes like it." He looked at her, to gauge her reaction, to shock her, to push her away—who knew why. A myriad of reasons why.

Kesley kept her face carefully composed. "Really?"

"Yeah, really. But I ain't gay. I ain't even bi. When I couldn't find a job, it was either do guys or sell crack, and I ain't selling that poison."

She nodded. "I'm glad you're not dealing."

"But the other, going down on men, disgusts you, huh? You think I'm disgusting."

"I think nothing of the sort. But I do think what you're doing is potentially dangerous. To your health. To your emotional frame of mind. Prostitution is also illegal. And John," she said carefully phrasing the next, "it doesn't matter crap what I think about you and what you're doing. It only matters what you think about yourself and what you're doing. At The Shelter, one of the services we provide is job counseling– "

"Too late for me to hold down a regular job."

"It's never too late There's more than one way to go through life, and most roads don't run straight and smooth. You've just taken a detour. The Shelter can help you get back on track."

Kesley took a deep breath. Pushing would only drive him away. "Anyway, I'm here to remind you about your follow-up Health Screening appointment. I'll go with you if you like…"

"Naw. I'm good."

Kesley stepped back. "I'll let you get back to your friends."

He nodded. "Goodnight Miss Richmond. And thanks."

With that, John Smith rejoined his group, and Kesley made her way back to the van.

◆ ◆ ◆

The next day, Kesley got the news. John Smith had kept his second appointment with the Med Van. As it turned out, he was clean. In fact, heathwise, the teen was in fairly decent shape. No chronic illness, no drug dependency. Yet. The volunteer internist on staff thought he had told the truth about his age too. Though too skinny for his lanky height and in possession of a fresh baby-face, John was nevertheless either eighteen or close to it.

Young, and not yet hardened to the life of a male hustler, John had a good chance of making it. The next time she saw him, she planned on offering him a whole range of opportunities. With options, he might get it together. With support systems in place, John might even become one of The Shelter's success stories.

The phone rang as she walked by it on the way to her kitchen.

"Hello," she answered, using her professional voice.

"Hullo yourself, me pretty."

Drew

Wait a minute—Drew never called her on the phone. Had something horrible happened?

"What's wrong?" she rushed out.

"Nuthin'"

"Then why are you calling me on the phone?"

"Just because. I know you just got home, and I wanted to talk."

Kesley twirled a strand of hair around a finger. "Talk? Talk about what?"

"Nuthin'"

Kesley took a deep calming breath. "If you wanted to have a conversation about nothing, why not simply open the door, like you always do, when I walked past your landing? Or, you could have followed me up the stairs, same as usual. Or, you could have emailed me. Are you feeling all right? There's a lot of junk going around. Colds. Fevers. People doing stupid things." She held out the receiver and glared at it in emphasis, and then calmly and rationally replaced it against her ear.

"Okay—here it is. This phone call is what you might call an experiment. I wanted to pretend we're like every other couple just starting to get to know one another. And about sending you an email—emails aren't real friendly. In an email, you can't listen to the emotional nuances in the other person's voice. And I hate those damn smiley faces. Is that what human beings have come to—using emoticons? Do you really want us to substitute little circles with humanoid characteristics to denote our feelings?"

Kesley held the receiver out about a foot or so in front of her face and shook it hard, and then replaced it once again against her ear. "You're nuts, you know that?"

"Sweetheart, we never talk on the phone, and that's what people who date normally do. We could both use the practice. So, let's practice. I'll go first, how's that?"

Drew sounded anxious, and he was never nervous, especially not in social situations. The man didn't have an awkward bone in his perfectly put together body. Frankly, because he didn't care about customs or rituals, he showed very little restraint when it came to breaking societal rules. His freethinking approach to life had always appealed to her. Now this—

"Here goes," he said. "Hi, Kes How was your day?"

"Awesome. Wait 'til you hear what happened at work…"

She caught herself in the nick of time.

Their agreement. They couldn't talk about work. Not for the next two weeks.

"Drew, no fair You're trying to trick me. We can't talk about work, and the job is the major portion of my day."

And the major portion of my life too.

"Sweetheart, you said your day was awesome. Quit holding out! I want a piece of that."

"You'll have to settle for a piece of me instead." She gave an evil laugh.

The voice on the other end went deadly serious. "Why can't I have both?"

"Because you can't. So, what do we talk about instead?"

Silence. Complete and utter quiet coming from the other end of the phone. If she didn't know better, she would think she had hurt Drew.

Impossible to hurt Drew. The guy had hippo-thick hide. Everything bounced right off him.

Finally, after listening to nothing for a few seconds, seconds that felt like an eternity to Kesley, Drew finally offered, "I'd like to go out with you. Would you please accept my invitation for dinner and dancing at Claudette's on Saturday night?"

His formality gave her a case of the giggles. "Are you serious?" she sputtered.

"Absolutely. I'm asking you out on an official date. The kind where I come knocking on your door and we go out to eat at a place that requires a tie and reservations."

She sobered. "But Claudette's. That's where couples go for special occasions. Birthdays and anniversaries and engagements. We're talking valet parking here."

"Since neither of us owns a car, that won't be a problem."

"What about the linen tablecloths?"

"I promise not to spill the wine. Better yet, we'll order champagne. It doesn't stain. How's that?"

"No plastic forks and knives?" She shook her head. "Actual silverware...?"

"I promise not to steal any. Any other caveats?"

"None. We're going dancing. Whoopee" Like a complete dope, she twirled around the floor of her apartment.

"Oops" Her twirling came to an abrupt halt. "Hold on a sec, Drew. I'm tangled up in the telephone cord."

"Lucky cord. I envy the cord."

She waited to get punk'd.

"I'll pick you up at seven," he said and hung up the phone.

Chapter Ten

On Saturday night, Drew was ready at quarter to the hour. Showered, combed, shaved and dressed, as shined and polished and spiffy as he ever got. With nothing left to do, and too wound up to watch the tube, he watched the clock instead.

Not much action going on between the minute hands, he thought, restlessly prowling his empty flat. Geez! Was he ever glad Kes couldn't detect his pacing footsteps upstairs on the third floor.

Ordinarily, if they were going out for a night on the town, say to a movie, he'd beat it up the stairs early and talk through the door at Kes while she changed from one pair of jeans into another—her work denims into her after-hours denims. He couldn't do that tonight, because this was their first official date.

Which also explained why they wouldn't be hitting the movies.

According to those in the know—magazine article writers—movies were a bad choice of entertainment for the first date. According to those articles, the first date was when a guy and girl talked, the kind of getting-to-know-you dialogue that made or broke the chances of getting that crucial second date.

Drew never went out on second dates, mainly because he never dated— at least not according to the article's narrow definition of what dating entailed. But he could understand the writer's logic. He'd been to plenty enough movies with Kes to know that when she stopped crying—she blubbered during every film, even comedies—she'd move right on from nose-blowing over the plot to arguing about the plot.

Creating yet another problem.

He never remembered the storyline. But to make Kes happy, he'd always—just for the sake of discussion—make up various plot points. Since those points never jived with what had actually happened on the screen, he ended up getting in trouble.

His sweetheart grooved on discussing stuff like foreshadowing, denouements and characterization, and he grooved on making her happy, so he honestly tried to stay awake. But once those lights dimmed in the theatre, man, staying conscious through to the closing credits was pretty much a losing battle. Darkness was for sleeping. End of story.

Which explained why they were going dining and dancing, not heading to the movies.

On their first date, there would be no sleeping. No trumped-up arguments based on faulty, made-up premises. On their first date, he was determined that they would have important dialogue, meaningful and riveting and revealing give-and-take conversation.

Already, the pressure was getting to him. Kes had better know how to conduct an interesting first-date-dialogue, because he had not a clue.

Clammy sweat broke out on his back. The drops slithered down his spine. The minute hand on the damn clock refused to move and he was beating the same boring path on the floor.

He wished his floor were longer, maybe with a few scenic wonders thrown in, just to break the monotony of pacing.

At five-to-seven, Drew could take the waiting no more. He picked up the two items he had put aside and, taking baby steps, headed for his apartment door. Opened the door. Closed the door. Quietly, so as not to alert Kes he was en route, thereby ruining the whole element of first-date-arrival surprise. One shiny shoe after another, he made his way down the hallway to the staircase that led to the third floor.

Here, he dawdled. After looking at his watch again, only for like the zillionth or so time, he determined he was still early. To kill a minute or two, he patted his pockets.

Wallet?

Check.

Cash?

Shuffling the two items he carried under his arm, Drew removed the wallet from his pocket, emptied the contents into his palm, lined the cash up in like denominations on the flat-topped banister, and then refilled the wallet so that bills all faced in the same direction.

Hold on. Maybe, he should pay with a credit card, thereby avoiding the need to figure out the tip in his head, always a hit or miss computation with him.

He rifled through the plastic credit card section.

Yep, all there, gold and silver and bronze, along with a photo of Kes.

Okay, more than one photo. The whole damn photo section contained nothing but pictures of Kes. Ten in all, one photo for every year he'd known her. She hadn't changed much since college. The hair length maybe, but that was about all.

Drew smiled at his collection.

Kes took great pictures. She never held back for the camera lens. Her face was open and honest and self-confident. He loved the way she let him see her, the real her. He loved the way she opened up for him in a way he never could bring himself to open up for her. He loved her laughing eyes, her pretty nose, her animated, mobile lips. He loved—

Kes.

Everything about her. There wasn't a single thing about her he didn't love. Most of all, he loved her quirks. Her foibles. The personality ticks that made her who she was. He wouldn't have her any other way.

Drew refilled his ass pocket with his wallet. Though he wanted to race up the stairs, he forced himself to slow down, to climb the stairs one at a time. Otherwise, he'd arrive too early and spoil everything.

Man, was he wired or what?

The clothes didn't help. He never wore a jacket and tie. Everyday was dress-down day in the company he owned. Unwilling to make his employees toe a line he had no intention of toeing himself, business dress in his operation was strictly do your own thing.

Not tonight. Tonight he wore a jacket and a tie and a brand-new white shirt that still had that department store stiffness, an outfit Kes had picked out for him a couple of years back. He also had on socks. Boxers too.

Christ. A date. What was he doing going out on a date?

At the third floor landing, Drew shifted the stuff he was carrying beneath an arm so he could knock on the door.

He rapped. A good one, all five knuckles.

Man, Kes had a hard door. Who knew?

Not him. He'd never knocked on it before.

"Come in," she called.

Drew stood his ground. It was important they followed the dating regulations, and that meant she had to come to the door and open it up before he stepped inside. Anything else was improper. For the past ten years, he'd been way impolite and he had a lot of improper to make up to Kes. A decade's worth. He'd start with the small discourtesies and work his way up to the large rudenesses. His lack of a knock was symptomatic of his many improprieties.

Symptomatic. Would you listen to him? He was beginning to sound like a social worker, for fuck's sake Kes had started to rub off on him. This was huge. Monumental. Hopeful.

He grinned. Hey, maybe some of her other good stuff would start rubbing off on him too.

Before Kes got a peek at his irreverent expression, he quick-stowed the smile. "Good evening," he said, straight-faced when she opened the door.

Dating was serious business and should be treated with the proper solemnity due it. "Kes, you look sensational tonight."

He'd rehearsed what he was supposed to say all day, so it would come out sounding spontaneous. This was not to say Kes didn't look wicked good in her slinky red dress, but he wanted to do things right, say things right, and *wicked good* was not nearly formal enough. The magazine article said ladies liked hearing right away that they looked "sensational" so he figured saying Kes looked "sensational" was the way to go. Getting it out of the way at the door took some of the pressure off, just in case he waited for later to say it and then forgot.

"Very sensational," he repeated, on the outside chance she hadn't heard the first time.

"Thank you. That's kind of you to say." She nodded to the items sticking out from under his arm. "My goodness Are those for me?"

Shit. He had the attention span of a gnat. He'd almost forgotten the gifts.

"Yes. For you." In a move that had uncoordinated dweeb written all over it, Drew thrust the box and paper funnel at her.

"Flowers and candy! How thoughtful."

Leave it to Kes to know exactly what to do, what to say, while he was floundering. And then she took social etiquette one-step further and leaned over and kissed him. On the cheek. Christ, but the kiss was sweet. Warm too. Where had she learned to do something sweet and warm like that?

Her parents. Kes' parents were the nicest people. Genuine, through and through. They always made him feel right at home when he took their daughter upstate for a visit. He'd go more often, but renting a car was a pain in the ass.

"I've definitely decided to buy my own set of wheels." Drew divulged as the idea occurred to him. "Then we can visit your parents more often. We should go see them in the next two weeks. It's only right. A nice girl like you would want to bring her date home for the intros."

"Huh? My parents already know you." Kes went face first into the florist funnel. She took a deep inhale of the blossoms. "These flowers smell heavenly."

"Not as heavenly as you," he said manfully, sniffing the air around her. "And I like your folks. I don't care that they already know me—I'm telling them I'm taking their daughter out. Do things up proper. If you don't want to come, I'll visit anyway. It's the correct thing to do. I don't like the idea of sneaking around in the shadows."

"Sneaking around in the shadows? What sneaking? What shadows? You make us sound like two characters in a film noir. My parents know you live downstairs. They've always known. In fact, your presence downstairs makes them worry less about me upstairs alone."

"Well, I just want them to know they don't need to worry now that we're dating either. I mean to behave like a perfect gentleman."

"What" she yelled, sounding really pissed. "I don't need a perfect gentleman. I need a sex machine. You promised." She pointed a finger at him. "No backing out on the deal now."

Here they were, still standing at the door, and already he'd put his foot in it.

This was where those employee-relations skills he'd developed over the years came in handy. Enter diplomacy.

"I meant," he said, digging himself out from the mess he'd created, "I intend to behave like a *gentlemanly* sex machine."

She looked at him cross-eyed, and then started to laugh. "Okay. We'll go see my parents sometime in the next two weeks. Thanks for letting me tag along, Drew. Nice of you."

"Don't mention it. I don't mind sharing Momsy and Pops."

She shot him a smarmy look. "I'll just go put this lovely bouquet in water. You really shouldn't have gone through all the trouble."

"No trouble," he called after her as she left to hunt down the vase.

As was proper date behavior, he didn't follow her. Though tough to do, he refrained from dogging her heels from room to room, making idle, yet deeply erudite, even philosophical conversation about sports or the weather, pertinent stuff like that, like he usually did. Instead, as was proper dating behavior, he stayed put. As she hunted down the vase, he satisfied his need to be with her by hollering through the paper-thin walls. "I wanted to buy the flowers. You like flowers. You buy them for your desk at work every week, right?"

"We can't talk about work, Drew."

"But flowers are only work-related, once removed."

"We talk about my desk, I'll start free-associating and before you know it, we'll be talking about John—See what I mean? I'm doing it already."

"Sorry. My fault." He was blowing it. They hadn't even left the apartment yet and he was screwing things up. Fat chance he'd get a second date now.

For lack of anything better to do with them, he stuck his hands in his pockets, and tried again. "I was thinking of getting you a corsage to wear, but the magazine said to get a bouquet. Also, about the candy—I got a mixed assortment. Some have nuts. I'm supposed to tell you that. You know, on account of food allergies."

Kes came back out carrying a vase. The flowers looked pretty, but not as pretty as the woman carrying them.

"Drew, you know the only food I'm allergic to is butterscotch. You've seen me eat bag after bag of nuts at Fenway Park."

"Yeah, those Sox. What a team, huh?" he said conversationally.

Her mouth opened, then snapped shut. She looked at him oddly, like she didn't know what to make of him.

Okay, so his comeback wasn't the most original, but banter-lite was the best he could do. Trying had to count for something. Maybe if they left the apartment, the date would fall into place. "If you're ready, we can leave. Unless you have a wrap or something. It's breezy tonight." Weather was a great icebreaker on the first date.

Kes reached to her comfy, over-stuffed chair and picked up a gauzy cover-up thing. Before she could wrap herself up, he swiped the shawl from her hands and settled it over her shoulders.

Her bare shoulders.

Her creamy-white, bare shoulders. Her shoulders looked so smooth. Silky-smooth.

Because he couldn't resist, Drew skimmed his fingertips along the tops of those silky-smooth, creamy-white, bare shoulders.

One touch, that's all it took, and it was bye-bye control, hullo no-holds barred chaos.

He wanted Kes. And now that she had legitimized that desire, lust rushed him, nearly floored him, nearly knocked him flat on his ass. Man, he was going down for the count.

"Good thing I didn't go with the orchid," he gasped, fighting for air, fighting to keep his head, while wave after wave of need pounded him. "There would have been no place to pin the corsage on your sensational dress."

That's when Kes cracked up.

Drew didn't know what she found so funny, and that was okay. He grabbed on to her hilarity like a boxer clings to the ropes.

When she went out the apartment door, her laughter pulled him right along after her.

♦ ♦ ♦

After an interminably long and torturously silent meal, during which Kesley had to pull every conversational word from Drew's mouth syllable-by-agonizing syllable, her normally gregarious date put them both out of their misery with a question.

"Kes, may I have this dance?"

Once out on the polished floor, she soon realized Drew's stiffly choreographed question had been a foreshadowing of his stiffly choreographed dance steps.

She couldn't understand it. Usually, Drew enjoyed slow dancing.

Not tonight. Tonight, he was acting like a stranger who said all the right things, showered her with polite attention, and remained emotionally distant. He barely touched her on the dance floor, and Drew was always affectionate. Now that she needed his natural warmth, he was freezing her out.

Well, she'd had enough!

She tapped his shoulder as they glided around the floor. "Why are you holding me so far away? You're weirding me out."

"I'm tense," he finally admitted. "This is our first real date, and I'm trying to go by the book. Or, in this instance, the magazine. The article I read said we are not supposed to touch below the belt while we're dancing."

"FYI—I know you have a penis."

He two-stepped her away from the crowded floor, leading her into a dark alcove. "Kes! There are mothers here dancing. You can't say 'penis' in front of mothers."

"Oh, yeah? And how do you think mothers got to be mothers?" She glared up at him. "I believe they used a penis. I would like to avail myself of your penis too, not for reproduction, but for recreation."

"I told you, Kes—you can't say the p-word on a first date."

"Fine. I want your COCK," she bellowed. "How's that?"

"Fuck." He sent her a look of horror. "Now see what you made me say. A vulgarity, and on our first date. Shit. I'll never redeem myself now."

Was that a blush suffusing Drew's strong jaw?

It was a blush! Even in the dark, his cheekbones shone red with embarrassment. And since Drew wasn't bashful, that embarrassment could mean only one thing.

"You're not hard," she accused. "And you don't want me to know. When you hold me in your arms while we dance, you don't get aroused."

"Stop, Kes," he hissed.

But she refused to stop. "You don't have an erection, and to keep from hurting my feelings, you're keeping me at arm's length."

Drew yanked her close, and a substantial bulge met her belly.

"I've had a hard-on for you since I placed the wrap over your shoulders. But I wanted this date to be perfect…"

"It's getting there," she said grudgingly.

"You have such soft skin." He groaned. "And there's so much of it showing in your pretty red dress. The magazine article said I wasn't supposed to mention the color, in case I screwed it up, but I just gotta say, you look like a strawberry ripe for the picking in your pretty red dress, and I'm the one in charge of picking you, and that's a whole lot of pressure."

"Here's an idea—harvest me tonight and get it out of the way."

"You don't understand—there are steps we have to go through first."

"Bypass 'em," she countered.

After emitting a pained *oomph*, as if all the air had been sucked out of his body by a huge unseen vacuum, he lunged for her. His weight forced her shoulder blades back against the wall, and his mouth descended, sealing his mouth to her mouth. Their hands moved over each other, fingers alternately fluttering and plucking and thumping and grasping, as though they were playing every instrument in the band, including the drums. What they were doing to each other wasn't stilted or choreographed. In fact, the feverish petting in the darkened alcove was nose-bumping, head-butting, hip jutting clumsy. All the right parts prodded the wrong places, and then all the wrong parts prodded the right places, and the lack of synchronicity mattered not one iota, because the spontaneity had returned the real Drew to her, the uninhibited, irreverent, passionate man she'd always had the secret hots for. She couldn't be happier.

Until the animal wildness ended as fast as it had begun.

"Sorry." Drew moaned. "So sorry, I lost control."

His hand supporting her elbow, as if he were presenting her at a grand cotillion, he escorted her back towards their table. "That should never have happened there."

"Where should it have happened?" she asked breathlessly. "And can we go there now?"

He shook his head. "I think I need to take you home."

Drew picked up her wrap. "Here, Kes," he said apologetically. "You'd better put it on. I can't trust myself to touch you."

He had to be teasing her—

But no. Drew's expression looked tight. Strained. She hadn't realized until right then how much this favor cost him. The guy was a sex machine, always up for the next score. His loss of control had nothing to do with her. Not really. Drew probably hadn't had sex since he'd agreed to act as her coach. In the language of her lost boys at The Shelter—the unfamiliar abstinence had to be tripping with his 'nads.

She placed the wrap around her own shoulders. "You must have a high level of testosterone, huh?"

He looked at her, his features rigid, and said nothing. Tight-lipped, he took her home without touching her, in complete silence.

She felt cheated. And a lot annoyed. She missed her pal, the one who would carelessly sling his arm around her shoulders as they walked around the city, the one she could talk to about any and all subjects.

Except sex. And himself.

At the three-decker, just like always, he accompanied her up to the top floor. After keying the umpteen locks he had installed because their landlady, in his opinion, hadn't supplied enough, he wavered.

"Kes, at this point I read that the woman is supposed to decide if she'd like to invite her date in for a drink or coffee or...or..."

"Sex," she contributed.

"Well, yea*hhhh*—" He shook his head. "Check that I meant no. No! Hell, no! That's not proper first date protocol! But—but—I'd feel less worried if you'd let me come in and check things out before I leave, just like always."

"Huh? I'm not understanding this. Wasn't the deal sex and lots of it?"

"But sweetheart, like I said, we're in first date mode, not in sex mode, so I'm not putting the moves on you..."

She wished. When would he put the moves on her?

"...but no lie, I noticed some cigarette ashes on the way from the second to the third floor, and neither of us smoke."

No, but their nosy octogenarian landlady smoked like a chimney. She often left a trail of ashes when she let herself into their respective apartments while they were out for the evening—something Drew was too pure of heart to have figured out.

Just as well that Kesley had kept her mouth shut about their landlady's propensity for snooping. Now, she had an excuse to trap Drew in her web of sexual seduction.

"Sure," Kesley said, standing aside while her date preceded her into the apartment. "Come on in."

"All clear," he said, after checking each and every room. "Thank you for the enjoyable evening. I'll just say goodnight now."

With that, Drew raced past her through the open door and disappeared down the flight of stairs.

No goodnight kiss.

After quoting from a damn magazine article on dating all night long, he'd skipped the most essential ingredient of a date.

Steam hissing out of her ears, Kesley charged down the stairs after him. On the second floor landing, shaking with righteous indignation, she rapped on his door.

Drew immediately opened up. "Uh-oh. What'd I do?"

"It's not a question of what you *did*," she spat. "It's a question of what you didn't do. So now tell me what I did *you* didn't like." She jabbed her finger into his chest. "Start talking."

"You didn't do anything I didn't like. I like everything you do. And this is silly. I live right downstairs—you know I'm calling you again. I'll probably see you tomorrow…"

"Aha There it is."

"There what is?"

"The social lie. Guys always say they'll call, and then never do."

"I've never once told a woman I would call and then left her hanging."

"But you left me hanging tonight."

Drew scratched the square line of his handsome jaw. "How did I leave you hanging tonight?"

"You didn't kiss me goodnight at the door. No awkward moment when I wonder if you will, no nothing."

"We kissed earlier."

"Doesn't count. Only the awkward-moment kiss at the door counts. Didn't that dumb magazine article stress the importance of the awkward goodnight kiss?"

Drew examined his shiny dating shoes. "Yeah, but…"

"But nothing. That awkwardness is due me and I demand what I'm due."

"I wanted our first date to be special. Something to remember. I'm sorry I botched it." Drew spoke very low.

Which made her feel even lower. Because this was Drew. Kind, decent, caring Drew. He didn't represent all males, and it was unfair to take out all her past dating hurts and mishaps on him. Drew was unique. One of a kind. Their relationship was also unique and one of a kind.

She flung herself into his arms, and locked hers around his neck. "I'm the one who needs to apologize," she whispered tearfully against his chest. "I'm the one who botched everything. I'm sorry for being such a bitch."

He set her away from him. With two hands on her shoulders, he rasped into her weepy face, "You are never to speak negatively about yourself again, do you hear me? I happen to admire the way you go after what you want."

The ugly tears kept dribbling. "I don't know what's wrong with me," she bawled.

"It's the artificiality of all this. We can't go back to a first date. It's too late for that. We can only move ahead, and what's ahead is this."

He pulled her close again, took her lips, and just like in the dark recesses of the dance floor earlier that night, he kissed her hot and wet and edgy. Despite ten years of unbroken familiarity, she was unacquainted with this shattering aspect of them.

When it was over, they fell back against an adjacent wall, both breathing hard.

Drew whipped open his collar, and raked his hands through his golden hair. "I agree to trash the dating magazine, if you agree to forget this date ever happened."

She gave a weak nod.

He held out his hand. "Shake on it?"

To seal the deal, they did.

Chapter Eleven

Green Rain threw her arms wide in exasperation. "It's cool to sort through the clothes. That's why the bins are here. Help yourself."

"I don't know my size," John Smith muttered.

Kesley stood in the basement of The Shelter, just around the corner from where Green and John were talking. They couldn't see her, but she could see them, and yes, she was intentionally eavesdropping.

"Say what?" Green's hands slid to her solid hips. "Dude, what do you mean you don't know your size?"

John squirmed under Green's scrutiny. "My mom always picked out my clothes."

Green chortled. "What a mama's baby!"

"Yeah—right up to the day my old man blew her away."

Behind her corner, Kesley's eyes welled with tears.

In every runaway teen there lurked a sad story, and today she had just learned John Smith's. In one short sentence, he had encapsulated his background, a background he would never have shared with her, not this soon and maybe not ever. But comfortable with Green, he had divulged his heartbreaking secret.

"I'm sorry to hear about your mother," Green said. "Sometimes, I have me a big mouth."

True, Kesley thought with a sniff. But Green was working through it in therapy. And despite her occasional outbursts—brought on by anger over years of chronic sexual abuse by a distant family member—the teen had an enormous heart. If anyone could take the prickly John under her wing, it was Green.

Not that she was a pushover. Green was a proponent of tough love, towards herself as well as towards others. She never wallowed for very long in self-pity. She shed a few tears, said a few bad cuss words, then bounced back and got on with it. She expected others to do the same. In group, if those others didn't put it in gear, if they didn't move past their individual stumbling block, Green was the first one to give them a therapeutic boot in the seat of the pants.

"Your mom wouldn't have wanted you to go around with holes in your jeans," Green said, administering a therapeutic, if non-physical, kick to John's posterior. "She would have wanted you to fix up your sorry punk-assed self so she could be proud of you."

So saying, she eyed John Smith up one side and down the other. "Un-un-un. You are one skinny badass, and that's for damn sure. A thirty-one inch waist will be a little baggy at first, seeing you ain't nuthin' but skin and bone. But don't you worry none. After eating a few meals here at The Shelter, you'll more than likely pack on a few pounds. As to length, I'd say you take a 34-inch leg." Green grinned. "I got me a tape measure 'round here somewhere. Want me to give you a measure?"

John Smith turned bright red. "No!"

Everything was sexual to a teenage boy.

While Kesley watched, Green elbowed John aside and went at the bins herself, selecting some items, throwing others every which way.

This budding friendship was a promising turn of events. A runaway was more likely to stay put if he or she developed peer bonds. Green might be just the incentive John needed to get involved in some of the programs The Shelter had available.

Green looked up from her sorting. "So, what's your name, new kid on the block?"

"John Smith."

Green Rain hooted. "Yeah, right. And my name is just what it says on the tag too."

"Why shouldn't a person be allowed to pick his own name," argued John. "I like the name you chose for yourself. Green Rain is awesome."

"Yeah well, Prince beat me out of Purple Rain, so I chose the next best thing."

"Your name is unusual. Good unusual."

"Honey, I wish I could return the good vibe right back at you, but I cannot tell a lie. John Smith, your name is highly usual."

He grinned. "I was looking for something generic."

"And you found it, dude. The name on my birth certificate says May Ellen Johnson. Maybe someday, you'll let me in on what name you were given at birth."

"Maybe," said John noncommittally, his cool very much in place.

Green tossed a basic black tee shirt and multi-pocketed pair of black cargo pants at John. "Try those on in the dressing room." She nodded her braided head in that direction. "Afterwards, come on out and show me your look. Hear?"

"Snap," replied John, and sauntered over to the closet-sized cubicle.

While he changed inside, Kesley left her hiding spot behind the corner and joined Green, who was busy putting the clothing bins back in order again. "Thanks for showing John the ropes."

"No prob. That's what I get paid the big bucks to do," snickered The Shelter volunteer. As an aside, she mouthed, *He's cute. Nice too.*

Kesley gave Green a silent nod.

Now if John would only talk about the violent death of his mother, maybe his grief would get out in the open where it belonged, instead of turned inward in self-destructive impulses.

Like hustling.

When John returned, Green gave the outfit her seal of approval. "*Kewl.*"

"I second the sentiment," Kesley agreed.

He beamed. "I trust both your opinions. Thanks, Green. Thanks, Miss Richmond."

John Smith had just taken an important first step.

♦ ♦ ♦

After her usual chatty gossip with Mrs. Harris on the first floor, Kesley floated on air to the second floor, elated about John Smith's progress at The Shelter. As a result, she almost tripped over Drew, who was slouched against his doorjamb.

Even when slightly disheveled, and a little rumpled, he still didn't look a mess.

"C'mon in, sweetheart."

Drew shouldered the door closed after her. "Might just as well get it over with. Now's as good a time as any."

Was he talking sex? He wanted to have sex? Now? *Right* now?

She could use a shower. Her legs needed shaving. Her baby fine hair, easily two months overdue for a trim, was a sight. Her limp bangs kept flopping into her eyes, and not in a good way, not in a sexy way. Unlike Drew, she had looking a mess buttoned down tight.

Just to make herself feel worse, she glanced over at him again.

Drew's back was glued to the door, as though he needed its support. Something was wrong...

Stepping closer, she sniffed the air surrounding him.

Fumes.

She frowned. "Do I smell beer?"

"Hell, yeah."

Kesley craned her neck up at him—even slouched, he towered her. "You've been drinking?"

"Hell, yeah."

"Drew, you don't usually drink anything stronger than coffee during the week."

"Hell, no. I've been known to drink beer."

"When?"

"In my misspent youth." Raising her hand, he placed a kiss in the palm.

Her curled toes didn't prevent her from thinking—*Drew had a misspent youth?* He never talked about his younger years, misspent or otherwise. Sometimes she thought he jumped totally gorgeous off the cover of GQ.

"Maybe you should sit down, Drew, before you fall down."

"Hey, I can handle my hops." He dragged her closer.

She went without a fight. "Now that I'm noticing, your clothes look like you've slept in them. And frankly, you really do smell like eau de brewery. Pardon me if I'm a little concerned."

One red, bleary eye slid in her general direction. "Ever talk about me in your bitch and cry group?"

"I told you, I made everything up. If you weren't intoxicated, you would remember."

"I'm not in-in-intox—I'm not drunk. I only had two beers. For breakfast."

She folded her arms over her jacket. "I see. Only two beers. For breakfast. Then how do you account for the fumes?"

"Must've been the four beers I had for lunch."

"And dinner?"

"It was a liquid dinner."

"Not soup, I take it."

"Nope. Not soup. And not beer either. I changed poisons. Whiskey. Straight. Wanna swill some down with me?"

"No, I most certainly do not. Is something bothering you, Drew?"

"Who me? Hell no. I'm cool. I'm on top of the world. At the top of my game. Tip-top. Everything's going my way. Listen, do we have to go into this now? I'd rather tell you how pretty you look. As pretty and pure as the snow outside."

She wiped beads of moisture from her brow—their apartments had no AC. "Drew, it's ninety degrees outside, and not much less inside here."

"I was going for the imagery."

She laughed despite herself. "You know what? Maybe we should wait to have sex. Why don't we go get a cup of coffee and something to eat instead?"

He hung his head. "I hate beer. Tastes like piss. And whiskey rots your gut. People say if you drink enough you forget. Alcohol doesn't do it for me." He looked over at her. "Sex does. I'm sorry, Kes. That's the truth. It's your right to know."

"I gather you intend to use me tonight to forget?"

"Maybe we can use each other. You need the experience. I need a woman's softness. It's an even exchange. Not real romantic but there it is."

"All right, Drew. I'm yours for the evening. But are you up for this in your inebriated condition?"

"I'll manage. Somehow."

A more enthusiastic lover would have been nice, but what the heck, he'd seen her through some rough emotional times, about time she returned the favor.

"Let's go for it," she agreed, her hairy legs and limp bangs forgotten.

Drew unfurled his long, lean body and took a sluggish step. And lurched. "Look, sweetheart, maybe this wasn't such a good idea after all. You deserve better. You should have the world's best lover."

She didn't want the world's best lover. She wanted him. Slightly drunk Drew. For the first time, he needed her. Not the other way 'round.

She reconsidered that last thought. Maybe, he didn't need her. Not precisely. Not her in particular. But a woman. Drew needed a woman. She was a woman, ergo, Drew needed her.

"No," she said stoutly. "I do not intend to back down now. I'm determined to go through with this."

"D'termined?" he slurred. "D'termination will get you through a root canal. Maybe I won't be a stellar stud tonight, but even drunk, I'm better than gum surgery." He fingered her jacket's lapel. "I just wanted this perfect for you."

Her suit weighed her down. Suffocated her. All these layers of clothing, all these layers of professionalism, layers upon layers of barriers—she wanted them gone. She wanted nothing to come between them. She wanted his hands on her skin. His mouth on her skin. His skin on her skin. She wanted to feel only him.

When five fingers cruised under her jacket, found a breast, stroked the nipple, she could have cheered. He wanted perfect? Well, his touch felt pretty darn perfect.

"Kes, sweetheart, I've wanted to do this since I saw you prancing around in your wet tee shirt. Do you have any idea what you did to me that night? How hot you were?"

"Nope, but thanks for telling me now that you're plastered. And why the past tense? Am I no longer hot?"

"Oh, you're hot. It's the suit that's not hot."

"I had a meeting today," she said, explaining her bureaucratic look. "The suit can come off."

Drew took her up on the suggestion. Under the weight of its outdated shoulder pads, her boxy jacket dropped like lead to the floor.

"Better," he said. "Much better." Big hands now moved on her breasts, circling them, cupping them, lifting them.

They were average breasts, not too big, not too small. "The girls" received the occasional whistle from construction workers, fairly standard practice in the city. She certainly never took the notice personally. They were just breasts. Ordinary. Every woman had a pair.

They became more than just ordinary breasts under Drew's worshipful attention. He stroked the hardened peaks, and her eyes closed, closing out the world and locking herself in a dark cocoon of rapturous sensation. He pulled on her blouse, freeing the hem from the waistband of her skirt, and her own groan reverberated in her ears. "*Yessssss.*"

She needed this. God, did she ever need this.

Her blouse, carelessly discarded, joined the jacket on the floor, and she gave herself over to Drew.

His mouth. Lord! His gorgeous mouth! Nuzzling her neck while his hands caressed everywhere at once. His bristly cheeks rubbed like sandpaper back and forth over the slippery polyester of her slip where her breasts rose to a scant roundness above the cups. The rough friction felt blessedly good against her fabric-covered cleavage, better still on her sensitized naked flesh. She raked both hands through his thick blond hair as the moist heat of his mouth scorched her through the dual layers of slip and bra. Throat arched, she lost all sense of reason when he scooped her breasts out from their respective cups, slip first, then bra, and kissed her bared breasts deeply, one, then the other, before mouthing the tips.

Her nipples. Her engorged nipples. His mouth sucked hard on her nipples.

"Oh, Drew. Yes. Just like that. Don't ever stop."

She unraveled. Everything else but this moment, this very instant, falling away. She felt like a kid in a candy store, unable to decide which treat to sample first. With Drew, she was greedy, wanted to try them all, sample every delight, anxious to make each sweet swallow last. She'd waited so long for this. Why hurry it now? She didn't want the sensations to swirl past her in only one color, no matter how vibrant that color might be. She wanted to separate each unique entity, to enjoy it for what it was, each individual characteristic dissected and analyzed.

Drew was not of a similar frame of mind.

He yanked the slip down to her waist, one of the slender shoulder ribbons ripping in transit. Then impatiently unhooked and tossed her bra. His sensual mouth pulled and drew and gorged on her tender breasts, his teeth scraping back and forth across the nipples until she thought she would go out of her mind.

Analysis, dissection—ha! Both fell by the wayside. A scream rose up within her, and in complete abandonment, she gave herself over to him.

What? Why was he pulling away?

An overpowering sense of loss descended upon her when he raised his head. Air played across her wet and swollen nipples, cooling the rawness of her flesh but leaving the ache behind.

"Don't go," she cried. "Please don't go"

He didn't. Instead, he bit her. As his teeth sank into her nipple, she did scream then, crying out in frenzied pleasure. Knees giving way, buckling out from under her, she sank like melted candle wax to the floor.

He followed her down. Heavy, so heavy, on top of her.

So, this is how it will be, she mused. Mindless, rushed coupling on the interior hallway floor of his apartment. She was just another woman to Drew. Any woman. Any body. Any willing pair of thighs. A new conquest—

Maybe *conquest* wasn't an apt description. She was hardly putting up a battle to save her virtue. There was no question of willingness on her part. She was willing. Very willing.

"I can't wait," he slurred moistly into the crook of her neck, his hand kneading her breast as he mounted her there on the hallway floor. "I'm out of my head with wanting you. Fuck waiting for the new bed."

And that unpoetic and unpretty declaration, so fiercely spoken, made everything all right.

With her head thrashing back and forth on the pitted wooden floor, she shivered. Illicit chills ran up and down her body, as though she'd come down with a fever.

What he did to her! How he made her feel!

Evil man, he ignored her whimpers, as excitement without boundaries, without limits, taunted her from the near distance just beyond her grasp, growing stronger with every sweep of his fingers, with every stroke of his mouth. Teeth bared, she stretched towards that pleasure like she would a brass ring on a merry-go-round. A nameless wonder, a spectacular firework display, a torment of surrender. And she did surrender, wholly surrender, her writhing body waving like a white flag, trapped between two narrow hallway walls, trapped within the limited scope of her own sexual experience. Wanting more. Needing more. Demanding more than he was giving her.

"Do you trust me?" he rasped between increasingly drawn-out kisses.

"Yes."

"I've been thinking about this all day. How it would be with you. To be your first. I want to make it good for you but it won't be good, can't be good for a woman the first time. I've got no experience with virgins. None. And I don't want to hurt you and I don't know how not to hurt you. I'm scared shitless. That's why I had the beers. Since you propositioned me, I haven't been able to eat or sleep," he confessed, his caresses growing heavy, his voice slow and deep, his big body a dead weight, crushing her on the floor.

He sounded so bereft. His sad little speech broke her apart like a champagne glass thrown to the floor at a wedding feast. But bliss came in lying in Drew's arms on the hallway floor, tangled up in half-on, half-off clothing, listening to him voice his fears. He had made himself totally available to her. How could she not return the favor by doing the same?

"Oh Drew. I'm scared shitless too. But not about this."

But how naïve of her to believe she could pick apart the fibers of making love! Coming together was more than just a physical act—

Still--how to qualify caring and sharing and closeness and this terrible letting go of self?

Vulnerability in the face of pleasure. Pleasure in the face of vulnerability. The individual colors didn't matter. With Drew, the whole spectrum of hues came into play, some a flaming vibrant intensity, some a hushed palette of pastels. And it was beautiful, all of it. Not perfect. But magnificent, all the same.

To save time—she had to have him inside her *n-o-w*—she reached up under her skirt and yanked aside her underwear, the fragile panel seam tearing in the process.

For joy. She now owned a pair of crotchless panties.

Giggling, she opened her mouth to confess her naughty thought, only to discover the heavy breathing in her ear had turned rhythmic.

She shook him. "Drew?"

Her almost-lover answered with a snore.

Chapter Twelve

Drew moaned. Forget about wearing a ball cap today. No way would any hat fit. Overnight his head had grown to twice its normal size and had developed a strange knocking noise, sort of like a little person had crawled in through an ear, dragging a giant hammer, intent on building him one whopper of a migraine.

Ignoring the pounding, he cocked an eyeball in the general direction of his feet. Experimentally, he tried resettling his ankles, wiggling his toes, shifting his heels.

Nothing happened.

Confused, he contemplated his size twelves. How come all that effort hadn't budged his loafers?

Uh-oh. He couldn't feel his feet. Someone—maybe the midget in his head with the hammer—had snuck into his apartment during the night and stuffed his loafers with someone else's feet. These dead feet weren't his feet.

"What the hell?" he said trying to shuffle his legs from their pretzel-twist.

Swell. Couldn't feel his feet or his legs.

Curling at the waist, he slapped at both.

Ouch. He felt that.

Inside his pounding skull.

Dead feet, pretzel-twisted legs, an inflated balloon for a head—didn't matter shit. He had to get up. His bladder—whoa yeah, now *that* he could feel—told him he had to take a leak. After making like a racehorse, he'd grab a shower, shave and dress. Maybe go in search of his missing brainstem…

Fire ants ran a race from his feet up to his knees, then morphed into sharp pins and needles as he straightened his spine and lumbered to a sit on the floor.

He wasn't feeling so good.

"Crap" he grumbled, his steel-wool tongue scratching out the word. Something told Drew he'd been a real bad boy the night before. The lingering memory of stupidity clung to him like mold on a shower curtain. What the hell had he done?

Had to involve a woman. Whoever she was, she was long gone now. The apartment had the usual vacant feeling, like nobody lived there, including him.

Not like him to pick up a woman when he was home. He never did the one-night stand routine in Boston. Never. Why last night? Sure, half-insane over the possibility of losing Kes, he'd tipped back a few malts. Sure, booze on top of no sleep on top of no food on top of desperation could do strange things to a man's reasoning abilities. But that didn't excuse him from getting on top of a woman and behaving like a jerk.

Speaking of which—why hadn't he just jerked-off?

Whenever he felt the call of the wild he always jacked the monkey, going solo being preferable to bringing someone back with him to his apartment, because, for fuck's sake, Kes lived right upstairs and he didn't want to offend her with sex.

At that last thought, Drew hauled his sorry ass upright and spied what he had used the night before for a pillow.

Underpants.

Not just any underpants. White cotton underpants. The modest type women he dated never wore.

Like they were rigged to explode, he bent and touched the panties.

Kes. The panties belonged to his sweetheart.

A deep, dark, pained rumble started at the rear of his throat and worked its way to his mouth where it exited on a sobbed, "No!"

The torn crotch on the panties confirmed his worst nightmare. What a prick! He'd been rough. With Kes.

About ready to puke, he remembered stooping to take her soft lips. He remembered the need to take care—

Drew wiped a shaky hand over his mouth. Some care he'd taken. He'd ripped her underwear.

Unable to wait, unable to stem the urgency, he recalled moving in on her, backing her up against the hallway wall. When she'd fallen to the floor, he'd pinned her there. With his much larger, heavier body, he had held her down. Tiny, narrow-hipped Kes. He must have crushed her, hurt her.

Raped her.

Christ!

Had he taken care of her? Had he at least worn a condom during the assault?

Drew checked the floor.

No discards.

And in the shape he had been in last night, he knew he could never have made it to the trash.

Shit!

Fighting the cowardly urge to step back from what had happened, to protect himself as he obviously had not protected her, to walk away and leave it alone, Drew forced himself to own up to what he had done.

Without considering her safety or virginity, he had put it to Kes.

There had been women. Not all *that* many, but some. And every one of them had been in it for a good time, same as him. He never took advantage. Never made himself out to be something he was not. All his dates understood going in that he wouldn't be spending his life or even the night with them. Fun and laughs were all he had to offer.

He didn't recall any fun and laughs last night.

Round breasts. A soft and giving mouth. An achy sigh. A throaty cry.

A cold slick of sweat covered Drew's body. Fear coiled in his belly ready to strike.

Kes!

He had to find Kes. Had to explain. Apologize. Grovel. Beg for forgiveness. Cut off his dick and hand it to her. He wouldn't need it anymore, not after doing what he'd done.

But the whole time he heaved accusations at himself, the whole time he told himself he was lower than dirt, the whole time he vowed never to go near her again, a small voice inside his head had started gaining in strength. And that small voice said maybe, just maybe, if he threw himself on her mercy she might give him a second chance, and if she did give him a second chance, the next time, he swore he'd do it right. He'd spend the rest of his life making last night up to Kes.

Outside her third-floor flat, Drew hammered on the door, hollered her name through the keyhole. He did not turn the knob and walk in like he always did. Things had changed between them.

Kes called out a fancy, French, *"Entrez"*.

Knowing he had forfeited all former privileges, he entered her apartment like a visitor and followed the aluminum clang of banging pots and pans to the kitchen.

The woman he'd wronged stood at the stove. He swore if she threw the frying pan in her hand at him, he wouldn't even duck.

Drew was about to fall to his knees at her feet, when Kes dropped the pan onto the electric coil and said, "Pull up a chair."

Chin to his chest, he collapsed onto the nearest one. "I'm so sorry."

"You should be." No beating around the bush with Kes.

"I am sorry, sweetheart. I truly am."

"Oh, well. These things occur from time to time. Or so I'm told. Now what would you like for breakfast? Hair of the dog?" She chuckled.

He couldn't believe she was letting him off the hook so easily. He didn't deserve her absolution. Maybe Kes could forgive him, but he would never forgive himself.

He said contritely, "Drinking is no excuse."

"My understanding is that it is. And why the knock this morning?"

"Considering last night, a knock was called for."

"I'm over it already. It's not like it's the end of the world. So I'm disappointed." Her shoulders lifted into a shrug. "Limp happens."

"Limp? Who was limp?" He paused, considered. Alcohol did have that side effect. "I was limp?"

"Guess so."

"What do you mean 'guess so?' Erect, I'm an impressive sight."

"If you say so."

"Huh?"

"I never got a gander at the goods. You were too intoxicated to unzip."

"I didn't?"

"Not even close. And by the way, you snore."

His head throbbed. His face hurt. Blinking? Pure hell. Despite the pain, his smile muscles flexed. "I do?"

"Like a bear in hibernation."

His smile exploded. "I'll make it up to you, Kes. I promise."

She slammed another pan on the stove. "No need. We'll only be together as a couple for a short while. I'll just wear earplugs in bed."

"I didn't mean the snoring. I meant that business about me being...you know."

"Limp?" she helpfully supplied.

"Yeah. About that. I'll make it up to you."

"I know you're good for it. And now that the grumpy look is wiped off your face, stay and have breakfast with me. I'm having a bowl of healthy oatmeal."

His nose wrinkled.

"You know, Drew, you're always after me to eat healthy. To skip the double servings of cholesterol and processed sugar and get back to nature. And now you have the audacity to wrinkle up your nose when I suggest you share a nutritious breakfast with me?" She sighed as she dumped the lumpy beige glop inside her breakfast bowl. "I just got back from shopping. Same as always, you'll find the Fruit Frisbees, Choco Choo Choo's, Peanutbutter Puffs, and Marshmallow Clouds in the top cabinet."

Jumping out of his chair, Drew headed in that direction.

"That plastic squirt ring you've been waiting for is inside the box of Puffs."

"The red one?" He looked back.

Nodding, Kes picked up her spoon. "The red one. Better hold onto it this time. I went to the mat in the middle of the cereal aisle to bring that baby home. A thirty-something jock thought he had first dibs. He was *sooo* not correct. I took him easy."

Tearing open the top of the cereal box, he reached inside the waxed bag interior. "Awesome. You're the best." After holding up the red ring to show her, Drew poured the chocolate stuff into his bowl, then added the primary-colored balls from a second cereal box. Next, he poured on the milk.

Between oatmeal swallows, Kes said, "The guy I decked in the cereal aisle gave me his phone number. Seems he likes doms. As soon as I rid myself of my chastity, I'm calling him."

Like, Drew was letting *that* happen.

Kes had just told him he snored. Though she seemed oblivious to its ramifications, Drew knew this uncomplimentary remark meant she loved him. Nose hairs and snores, she'd said so herself, that no woman dumps that kind of information on an unsuspecting guy unless she loves him.

Kes loved him.

She just hadn't caught onto it yet. Unlike himself, who knew, who had always known, at least in some part of himself, that he loved her—

Over his spoon, Drew watched Kes eat her beige glop. In her green checked summer dress with a big white collar, her arms and legs sun-kissed bare, her short brown hair neat and shiny, she looked just as composed and determined and sure of herself as always.

Suddenly, keeping to the status quo of that *always* didn't seem nearly as appealing. Because if he didn't make a change, if he didn't move forward, guaranteed, the beautiful, perfect, confident woman who sat across the table from him shoveling oatmeal into her mouth would move forward without him.

Kes had the guts to go after what she wanted, and what she wanted was a mainstream future involving marriage and kids.

Mainstream. He didn't even know what that was. Didn't even know if he could fake it. But if he couldn't pull that trick out of his hat, he'd lose her.

At the thought of how bleak his future would be without Kes, Drew lost his appetite. While the woman he loved ate her wholesome breakfast, he stared down into his bowl as his favorite cereal turned to mush.

Chapter Thirteen

Kesley had only just finished transcribing her clinical notes when Denise poked her head inside the partially ajar office door. "Got a minute?"

"Always." Kesley motioned her friend and fellow social worker to take a seat.

While Denise plopped onto the vinyl-cushioned chair, carefully avoiding the sharp, pantyhose-snagging rip at the edge, Kesley opened the bottom drawer of her metal desk and propped her sneakers up on top. "So, is the nature of this visit professional or personal?"

"A little of both."

With a nod, Kesley reached into the coffee can located on the upper hand corner of her standard green blotter, and pulled out two pieces of cellophane-wrapped hard candy. One she kept, the peppermint, the other, the cinnamon, she tossed at Denise, who caught it with the skill of long practice.

A raspy throat was an occupational hazard of running therapy groups. Though the teens in the sessions did most of the speaking, sometimes they went off on non-productive tangents and had to be talked back on track again, thus the need for soothing hard candy.

"The kids got a little vocal today in group, didn't they?" Kesley unwrapped the cellophane and popped the candy in her mouth.

Denise did the same. "Vocal? I'd call it downright loud. I had to screech to get heard above the uproar," her hoarse friend replied. "Then again, the kids always do get loud when the subject is date rape. Guys on one side of the issue, gals on the other, both seeing the circumstance from their own particular gender bias. Lots of polarizing issues like that between the sexes."

Kesley heard between the lines. "Is that the personal or the professional part of our chat?"

Denise gave a half-hearted smile. "A little of both. Jim and I split. I wanted you to hear the news directly from me."

Now that Kesley thought about it, during their co-lead group that morning, Denise had seemed less animated than usual. Instead of asking what was wrong, Kesley had chalked up her friend's quietness to pre-wedding fatigue. She should have known something was wrong—all the indications had been there. Beneath all the talk of bridal gown selections and reception hall choices and possible destinations for the honeymoon trip, Denise hadn't seemed happy.

"I'm so sorry." Kesley reached for her friend's hand and gave it a brisk squeeze. "Anything I can do?"

"Help me make out the cards for the returned shower gifts?" Denise gave a dismal chuckle.

"If that's what you need…"

"I don't know what to write. Got a catchy limerick to explain calling off a wedding two weeks before the ceremony, something that will make the guests laugh?"

"I'm sorry, honey, I don't."

"That's okay. I'll think of something. Maybe on the order of—Jim is a nice person. Denise is a nice person too. They just don't want to make nice-nice together until death does them in…"

Denise looked out the office window. "I can't even cry. I feel like such a spoiled brat. Like a real ingrate."

Kesley kept her voice even. "Why do you say that?"

"Because, it wasn't like Jim was a no-good bum or anything. He *really* is a nice person. He never cheated on me or gambled or drank or did drugs or slapped me around, or had any other terrible vice. He was never mean or cruel or bad-tempered. And I know deep in my heart that he would have made a wonderful father. And I feel spoiled because, though Jim is a good man, a fine man, I wanted more."

Louisa Trent

Denise returned her sad eyes to Kesley. "Is that so wrong—to want more?"

Kesley shook her head. "No, it's not wrong. You shouldn't settle for less than what you need."

"I loved him and he loved me. But we never hurried back to one another. Not after work, not from the store, not from being out with friends. We never truly missed one another when we were apart. Isn't that odd? It's such a small thing, and yet so meaningful too. I wanted him to miss me, and I wanted to miss him. And we just didn't. We didn't *need* one another."

"Do you know why?" Kesley asked softly.

"I think—because we didn't complete one another. We were complete without one another."

"Being independent is a positive trait," Kesley offered.

"True. But not to the exclusion of the other person. We were doing that, shutting each other out. So we decided to go our separate ways before the wedding, rather than drift apart afterwards."

Denise re-crossed her legs. "I want, have always wanted, what you have with Drew."

"Pardon? *What Drew and I have?*"

"Yes, what you two have. I'm jealous of what you two have together. That indestructible tie that nothing can break. You enjoy his company over and above anyone else's and he enjoys yours the same. I've seen his eyes light up when you walk in a room. He doesn't see anyone but you."

Now Kesley was shocked. "You have the wrong idea. Drew and I aren't, have never been, a couple."

"No?"

"Certainly not Not the way you mean. We don't have those sorts of feelings for one another."

"Don't let Drew get away."

Kesley laughed. "Drew has a different woman in every port."

"And he comes home to you. Hurries home, rushes back...to you."

"That's not the way it is, Denise."

"Kesley, sometimes we social workers know everything about everyone else and know nothing about ourselves."

What was Denise driving at? And how had the conversation turned to Drew and her?

Her friend rose to her feet. "Do you remember the time Drew left on one of his business trips, and you lost his contact information? This was years ago, before everyone started carrying a cell phone or a beeper. You were frantic when Drew didn't call, like he usually did."

"Yes, I remember that comedy of errors," Kesley said, taking a side trip down memory lane. "Funny now, not so funny then."

"You had him lying sick someplace. As it turned out, he had been calling and leaving messages, which you never received because your answering machine was out of commission."

"That's right," Kesley conceded. "And when he finally did reach me here at work, I lit into him on the phone." She chuckled. "What I didn't say to him!"

"Yeah, and knowing how upset you were, he cancelled the remainder of his meetings and flew home. Early. Didn't Drew lose an important account because of that?"

"Yup. And I felt terrible. But that's not the same thing..."

Denise shook her head. "Regardless, I want that, Kesley. I didn't have it with Jim. And to be fair, Jim didn't have it with me either. So, we took the mature action and admitted it. The breakup was all very amicable, and we're still friends. We'll probably stay in touch for a while, but eventually we'll stop making the effort—and it *will* take an effort—and then we'll never hear from one another again."

"I still don't see how this relates to Drew and me..."

Denise walked to the door. Before opening it, she turned back. "John Smith is downstairs playing ping-pong in the rec hall."

Hope soared inside Kesley. Hanging out at The Shelter was a start, but the teen runaway needed to enroll in a scheduled program, something structured.

Jumping out of her chair, Kesley followed Denise out into the hall. "I think I'll go watch a little ping-pong."

Chapter Fourteen

Drew leaned his backbone against the doorframe, watching as his sweetheart come dragging up the stairs, her usually optimistic face wearing a defeated look.

"Hey you," he yelled down the treads at her. "Why so glum?"

"How do you know I'm glum?"

Just like Kesley to answer a question with a question. "The upside-down smile was the tip-off. Have an upsetting anger management session?"

"Do you know my group schedules for every day of the week?"

Another question. Kes was just full of them tonight.

Sticking out his chin, so she could land him one easily, he said, "As it so happens, yeah, I do keep track of your schedule. What of it?"

"Oh, nothing," she said listlessly.

Kes backing off? Kes not wanting to square off and go a round with him?

This worried Drew.

"C'mon," he cajoled. "Get your shapely bottom in here and we can talk."

"Can't," she murmured, not looking at him. "Not tonight. I have a bunch of notes I need to write up."

While Kes avoided him, Drew searched her face. Took in the shadowed eyes, the too pale skin, the tight look around a normally lush and giving mouth, the whole pinched appearance of her features. Then, he noted her rounded shoulders—from carrying the weight of the world. His sweetheart had taken a direct hit today.

Dammit. He couldn't stand seeing her look so defeated. He wanted to take care of her And it slayed him that she wouldn't let him.

"Did you remember to eat dinner?" he asked softly.

"Drew, you are not my mommy."

He clutched his chest.

"Quit the playacting, Drew," she snipped. "I know I didn't wound your pride—"

What pride? When it came to Kes, he had no pride. And it would take a hell of a lot more than her disrespecting his masculinity to get him to back off.

In the past, he had tried to push her away, and she had never once budged. Not an inch. His turn now to be there for Kes. To maybe take some shit from her. Big deal. He could handle shit-taking. No matter what happened, she was not shaking loose of him. No matter what she did or said, she was not driving him off. He could handle anything...except losing Kes.

"Whoa. Where'd all the hostility come from?" he asked, trying to jolly her out of her funk. "Are you channeling teenage angst or something?"

Normally, at a crack like that, Kes would have given him a wry smile or a flip comeback. Normally, she would have regained her sense of humor and laughed at the sometimes ass-kicking irony of life. Then, after they talked it out, she would have moved past whatever had bugged her at work.

This time, Drew could see there was no moving past what had upset Kes

This was serious. Some kid was in trouble, deep trouble, and though Kes was knocking herself out trying to reach him or her, this time she wasn't pulling off the magic feat.

Magic—that is what she did. Either that, or a miracle. There was no other way to describe what she accomplished with those kids. No way to scientifically explain it. Yeah, she had a bunch of academic credentials after her name, but to his mind, that wasn't what kids responded to in her. To his way of thinking, troubled kids responded to her willingness to go to the mat for them, to pull out all stops, to sacrifice even her own health and strength and happiness for them. Drew admired that quality about her...and that quality also drove him nuts.

"Sorry," she mumbled from some dark place. "Guess I'm tired. And yes, Drew, actually I did forget to eat. Mainly because I wasn't hungry. But thanks for asking."

Time for a dose of reality. Even saints have to eat, and even halo wearers can't save the world on an empty stomach. Little troopers need fuel to keep soldiering along.

"I'll make you a sandwich," he coaxed, *hell yeah*, just like her mommy. And he didn't care if that's how he came across.

Grilled cheese oughta do the trick, he thought, planning the menu. Comfort food, easy on the digestion, not much chewing involved. Kes would feel better once she had something in her belly.

"With soup," he added. Stick-to-the ribs, easily tolerated, tomato soup.

She shook her head. "I just can't. I'm sorry."

That needless apology moved him past worried, into just plain scared. "You gotta have some down-time, sweetheart. Do your note writing tomorrow."

"There won't be time tomorrow, I have meetings all day. Besides, I want to put down all my thoughts tonight while they're still fresh in my mind."

"What thoughts?" He reached for her shoulder and found tightly clenched muscles under his fingertips. "Tell me."

"Talking about him won't help."

Aha. First clue. The kid in trouble was male.

Some snot-nosed whelp had gotten Kes all tied up in knots so bad she couldn't eat or sleep or play. If Drew found out who was making his girl miserable, he'd give that runaway something to bellyache about but good—

Impulses like this explained why he'd steered clear of social work as a career path. Made a hell of a lot more sense for an edgy guy like him to make a truckload of money so he could write out large checks and distribute them to those professionals more temperamentally suited to help. With that said, he did have a basic understanding of how a young male in trouble thought, and he did know a little something about teen runaways.

"Sweetheart, why not just paint the kid's problem in broad strokes? Sometimes, just having to explain the situation to a listener helps bring solutions to light."

"Nope. Getting away from the problem will give me some much-needed perspective, and then maybe I'll find a solution all on my own."

He rubbed her muscle-knotted shoulder. "How's about I give you a massage then?"

She cocked a defiant brow at him. "The only massage I want involves nudity and sex oils."

"You really think that's a good idea?"

"You told me you use sex to forget—why can't I?"

She'd just issued him a challenge. Swell.

Kes was strung out, probably operating on zilch for sleep, functioning on raw nerves and no food, and oh yeah, she was a virgin too, and he was supposed to whip it out and show her a good time?

Yeah. Right.

He'd need to have his head examined to even consider it.

The pathetic thing was—he had considered it. And she was damn right to remind him that yeah, he did, from time to time, use sex medicinally. A round of dirty sex would go a long way towards busting her stress levels and bringing on a good night's sleep.

Sex as a muscle-relaxer. Sex as a sedative. Sex to bring on forgetfulness. Hey, he had snoozed after random fornication for years. Sex could do it for her too—

If she had some experience, which she didn't, which meant he wasn't breaking out the sex oils, not tonight.

Still, he wasn't opposed to letting her work out her frustrations on him. No oils, and they'd keep their clothes on—neither dumb nor noble, he knew getting with her naked would lead to more. But, hey, a few kisses, some petting, wouldn't kill him.

Not too much, anyway.

A big boy like him could live with achy testicles.

Drew leered at Kes. "Step into my massage parlor, sweetheart, and I'll see what I can do."

She shook her head. "I told you, not unless we strip each other's clothes off and get out the scented oils. And no sense trying to fool me here—I know that's not what you have in mind. What you have in mind is giving me one of your famous backrubs. And I appreciate the offer and the sentiment behind the offer, I really do, but I have this embarrassing little impediment I need to lose and a chaste massage won't do it for me."

"Kes, sweetheart, you're tired—"

"Say no more. I understand. And the rational part of me knows you're right—I am tired and tense and cranky too. Tonight probably wouldn't be good for either of us. Bad enough sticking a virgin on you without palming off one who's also bitchy and uptight."

Turning and pushing away from him, she started for the stairs.

Drew was on her before she made it to step number three. No way was he letting things end like this between them.

"Get back here," he ordered, his knuckles seeming to sprout hair and drag on the floor. Kes might not realize it yet, but she was his, and no caveman worth his fur loincloth would let his woman go to bed hurting the way she was hurting.

She tromped back down to where he stood on the landing. "Yeah. So? I'm here. What do you want?'

"Hey, drop the 'tude, girl."

She fisted her hips. "I have things to do."

"Later. You ain't goin' nowhere now."

Two hands at her waist, he lifted her dainty feet clean off the ancient hallway linoleum, and set her back down on his leg, the foot of which he had braced on a step, thus sneakily converting a limb into an orgasmic sawhorse. In that position, he drew her forward to straddle his thigh.

As fate would have it, she was wearing a skirt. He yanked at the summery material so it puffed up around her middle leaving her, clad in cotton panties, riding his jean-encased thigh.

He kissed her ear, her jaw line, his tricky hands inching her blouse upwards from the waistband of her skirt. "Comfy?" he asked.

He never gave her chance to answer.

His mouth latched onto her mouth. His palm tunneled under her loosened blouse and cupped her breast over her bra. To his delight, she instinctively started to hump him.

Males, especially teenage males, understood and accepted the occasional need for behaving like a *dawg*. Ladies rarely admitted to a comparable need. He suspected Kes never masturbated, doubted she even knew how.

As Drew kneaded her dainty breasts, concentrating his efforts on those tight, mouthwatering nipples, he kissed her until he moaned. Unable to continue just kissing her, he tore his mouth off hers—

And made the incredibly stupid mistake of looking at his sweetheart's full, succulent lips, now reddened and swollen. He yanked his eyes to her eyes, which were glazed and heavy-lidded, kind of slumberous, her unfocused gaze sort of expectant, as though she were waiting for something to happen, something wondrous, something that maybe involved fireworks.

"Kes," he panted, "I have to…I have to…I gotta, you know…"

Only she couldn't know, and he couldn't explain, couldn't put the terrible need for her into words.

Letting action do the talking, he lifted her off his thigh, and touched her feet to the floor again. While she wove back and forth unsteadily, he backed her against the wall. One palm flattened to her breast, the other hand pulling at her skirt, he pressed his jean-covered loins to her panty-covered loins and did what he hadn't done since he was a teenager.

He started some dry-humping grinds. His pelvis to her pelvis, his hardness to her softness, his hurting bulge to her receptive hollow. With his mouth open against the side of her neck, his lips inside the unbuttoned collar of her feminine blouse, his nose inhaling the ladylike floral scent of her perfume, all the while ferreting out her natural scent, her distinctly female fragrance, he rocked into her. Pumping his hips, he performed a rhythm that had crazed written all over it.

Dry sex. Humping.

Flirties minus dirties. A naughty motion-without-the-lotion. Tubin', no need for lubin'. And Kes was fully reciprocating.

Christ Jesus They were going at it in the hallway like two pubescent adolescents.

Kes was the best, the best he'd ever had, no matter that they were both fully dressed. Groaning, grunting, no control at all, like a kid with his first girl, he lost it.

He'd never been so mortified. Or sticky.

Did Kes know? Could she tell what had just happened? And what was he supposed to say at an embarrassing moment like this?

"You okay?" he asked, finding it hard to meet her eyes, but manfully forcing himself to do it.

"Fine," she answered, and grinned.

His heart clutched. *She knew.* "Er—about what just happened…"

"I do declare," she said, fanning herself, "that was hot."

"It's better horizontal and naked. And mutual."

She tsked. "Drew, you do wonders for a girl's ego."

"Huh?"

"A few minutes ago, I was feeling whipped, and now I feel…well…empowered. Like I could tackle anything, any problem, and win."

"You go, girl," he said bleakly.

"Oh, lighten up. You just haven't had…" here, she had the unmitigated gall to chortle, "…release in a while, and I just happened to be handy. I don't think any the less of you because you popped your cork without the benefit of a champagne glass."

"Cheers," he said glumly.

As if champagne bubbles tickled her nose, Kes started giggling. Boneless with an attack of the sillies, she held onto the banister for support and doubled over.

He'd been going for loosening her up, getting her to relax. She looked plenty loose and relaxed now.

Straightening up, she blew him a kiss and raced up the stairs. "Suddenly, I'm absolutely famished," she hollered back at him. "I'm making something to eat and then calling it an early night. Thanks pal. I needed that."

"Yeah," he grumbled. "Don't mention it. Anytime."

Chapter Fifteen

Eight p.m. came and went and John Smith had yet to arrive at his assigned anger management group. As Kesley watched the door, hoping against hope that the runaway teen with the heartbreaking past would walk in late, her frustration and yes, anger too, escalated.

The streets had won before, and though each rejection hurt, she had never before lost her professionalism. Why now?

She didn't understand why she felt so depressed, so devastated at the thought of John turning his back on what she could offer—

Delete that.

She didn't understand why she felt so depressed, so devastated at the thought of John turning his back on what The Shelter could offer.

Stop personalizing the rejection, Kesley.

But she had to validate the feeling, accept it as real, own it, even if irrational. She did take his rejection personally.

John Smith reminded her of someone. Who, remained a mystery. All she knew was—she couldn't let him go. Not without a fight.

So, after he no-showed her anger management group, she went out on outreach alone, and on foot, looking for him.

Though the action was dangerous and foolhardy, her sanity compelled her to reach out to John Smith one last time. He was on the skids and she couldn't turn her back and let it happen.

In a public park, she found him soliciting sex. When she got in his face, which interfered with his business in a very real sense, he promised to attend her next session.

John's future balanced on the cusp. He could go either way—transition into a program or hitch a ride out of town. She too walked a fine line between reaching out and nagging. Too little advocacy and kids slipped through the cracks, too much pressure and kids stopped listening and tuned out.

After doing all she could to convince him to come in off the streets, Kesley had no choice but to leave the young prostitute to his customer.

Busy with John and two other teens in crisis, while dealing with the trickle-down repercussions of a slow economy—the budgetary crunch translating to cutbacks in services at The Shelter—she ended up having to cover her own caseload and uncovered emergencies, as well. Consequently, she hadn't been home in three days. And consequently again, she remained a virgin.

And time was running out.

Ted had left her a message on her apartment's answering machine—could they discuss setting up a date?

In all her frantic busyness, she'd missed the weekly bitch-and-cry session. Returning his call from work, she'd given him a resounding "yes".

A nice man like Ted was not slipping through her fingers. The date might be the start of a promising new relationship and she intended to go for it. No more taking a pass on the future. She was a traditional woman with a traditional woman's aspirations. If wanting a husband and family was no longer fashionable, too bad. Those goals worked for her.

The trolley let Kesley off at the corner of her street after midnight. She started the short walk to her apartment. Deep in contemplation, she made her way down the sidewalk under the city streetlights.

An SUV pulled alongside her and stopped.

Startled she looked up. "Drew!"

"Get in," he said through the open passenger door.

Ducking her head into the interior, she inhaled the unmistakable smell of new leather. "This car isn't a rental, is it? You did it. You actually went out and bought your own set of wheels. I don't believe this!"

"I said get in." Leaning to the right, Drew extended a long arm across the seat and pulled her inside, slamming the door shut afterwards. "From now on, if you're staying late at work, I'll pick you up. No more walking home alone at night from the trolley stop."

Her pleasure at seeing him after a three-day absence quickly boiled to anger. Where did he get off telling her what to do? She could take care of herself, and he knew it.

Still—she kept her tone reasonable. "I always take the streetcar."

"That was before we hooked up."

"Did I miss something here? As far as I know, we haven't had sex yet." And so what if they had? Did making love suddenly turn a smart woman stupid? She could fend for herself.

"I had my mouth on your mouth. I had my hand on your pussy. I tore off your panties. What do you call that?"

"Foreplay. And I was the one who tore off my panties." She took a calming breath. "Drew, I never took you for the possessive type. Is this how you behave with all your women?"

"No. Never. I'm never around long enough. Sometimes I don't even know their names, never mind where they live or work, so possessiveness is pretty much a moot point."

"Pretty soon, we'll be a moot point too."

"Let's stick to the present. As of right now, today, you belong to me and I belong to you. That was the deal."

"I know what we agreed on, but there are extenuating circumstances," she said hotly, reasonable gone.

"Talk to me, Kes, dammit!" He pounded the steering wheel. "Tell me what's going on. What are these extenuating circumstances?"

"The deal was—no talking about our respective careers."

"Then, take time off from work so we can do this thing right."

"I can't."

"Why not? Employees at The Shelter are entitled to a vacation the same as everyone else."

"I can't get away right now. It's not a good time."

"You're avoiding me, Kes. You offered me your body and now you're backing out."

"That's not so. I happen to have a date with Ted coming up in the near future, and I was only just thinking I needed to get on the stick and lose my virginity."

"To do that, you need to get on *my* stick."

"That's vulgar."

"That's real. I can't phone it in, sweetheart. I need to put it in. And we need to be together for that to happen."

She sighed. "How did you know I would be on that trolley?"

"I didn't."

"But…"

One-handing the steering wheel, he reached for her shoulder. "I've been meeting all the trolleys. You never called, never told me you were sleeping over at work, so I met them all. For the past three days, starting at 6 PM, I waited for every fucking one."

"Oh, Drew," she said softly, her anger dissolving. "I'm so sorry. I should have called. Frankly, I don't know why I didn't."

She shook her head. Why hadn't she called? She knew Drew would worry. She *should* have called. Obviously, more than one person in this car had been acting out of character lately. Why?

No idea. Here she dealt with the complexities of human motivation for a living, and yet she couldn't figure out her own.

His hand dropped away. "The bed arrived today." Drew looked straight ahead at the road. "It's all set up."

She nodded. "Ah. The bed." But he was driving away from the apartment, not towards it.

He cleared his throat. "I'm moving out, Kes."

"Pardon?"

"I'm moving out of the apartment and into a house I've rented. I'm getting all new furniture, the works. I'm junking the stuff left over from my undergrad days."

She was a remnant from his college days. Was he junking her, too? "You're renting an entire house?"

"Four bedrooms. Three baths. Fenced-in yard. The house has been vacant for a while, tied up in probate. An estate settlement. That's why I'm renting. But when the house goes on the market, I'm there with my checkbook. The dumpster is at the apartment now. Before I leave on this next assignment, all the trash I've collected over the years will be gone."

Including her, she supposed. He was trashing her. "This is happening so fast, Drew. There's a lot to absorb here. So many changes at once."

"Here's another. This is my last consult away from home. I've decided to take on the local work, stay in New England, let my employees start doing the traveling. I'm tired of airports. Thus my need for the SUV."

"You won't be away for weeks at a time?"

"Plants need care, Kes. Can't take care of 'em if I'm not around." He paused. "So—you wanna see the bed or what?"

"I want to see the bed. Can't wait."

"Good." He stared out the windshield.

"Fine." She looked out the passenger window.

In the frosty silence that ensued, Kesley examined her rumpled jeans, wrinkled shirt and grass-stained sneakers—the same clothes she'd worn for outreach. Her first breakout sexual experience and she was dressed in stale clothes. Not only that, she felt tired and stressed.

And Drew was angry with her. He had never been angry with her, not in the ten years they'd known one another. Why now?

"Do you want to talk, Drew?"

"No," he grumbled. "Do you?"

"No. Talking isn't what I want. Let's just tune everything out and have sex."

"It's not the best, you know."

"What's not the best?"

"Mindless sex. Not that I've ever had anything else. But my gut tells me, Kes, that there has to be more, you know?"

"Yeah, I understand about wanting more."

Drew slowed as they drove down the street that abutted Jamaica Pond. They were still in the middle of Boston, yet the area had a rural feel to it. The houses were well-maintained, the grounds nicely landscaped with bushes and flowers and majestic trees. Kesley had always considered this part of Boston the best of all possible worlds, country living yet within close proximity of all the wonderful cultural opportunities the city had to offer, not to mention the area's convenience to schools and hospitals. She'd told Drew many times that if she could afford the pricey real estate market, this locale is where she'd want to buy a house. Of course, on a social worker's salary she'd never own property anywhere, never mind in this swanky area.

"What a fabulous neighborhood," she said, still gawking out the window long after Drew cut the engine.

"I'm glad you approve. The slate-shingle roofed house over there, the one directly under the streetlight, is mine."

"It's wonderful," she exclaimed as he opened the passenger door.

"The driveway is double width, built for two cars. No more towing worries."

Why was Drew making such a big deal about the width of a driveway? And why park at the curb? As if he presented the place for her inspection?

She lost that train of thought when he keyed the lock of an arched oak door with a leaded window reminiscent of a medieval castle. "How beautiful!"

Drew stepped inside the foyer, Kesley following. "The power hasn't been turned on yet," he explained. Striking a match, he lit a candle, placing it on the entryway windowsill. "And there's no place to sit. Only the bed."

"The lack of a snoopy landlady more than makes up for the furniture deficit." She looked around the huge empty rooms. Gosh, she'd love to decorate all this empty space. Drew always teased her when she drooled over home magazines, and now he'd gone and bought an empty house, just waiting to be given a personality. These vacant rooms could easily be transformed into a warm and inviting home.

"Drew—would you be kind enough to direct me to the powder room? I'd like to take a shower. First."

The blush crept up on her. She talked about sensitive sexual issues all the time to the kids she counseled and never even blinked. Now, she felt bashful.

"Right this way," Drew said, not bashful at all as he led her to the bathroom, setting the candle on top of the vanity sink—*Drew with a vanity sink!* "I did stock up on the essentials, so you'll find clean towels to your left. Oh, and as an extra perk, the toilet doesn't overflow."

She was still chuckling when the door closed. After undressing, she turned on the shower and stepped into the tub, shutting the glass enclosure after her.

A quick shampoo and a scrub, and she toweled off. Fortunately, her hair sported a wash and wear style. After brushing her teeth with some toothpaste applied to a finger, she was ready for her deflowering.

Having no robe, and thinking a towel silly, she left the bathroom naked and carrying a candle.

She bumped into Drew in the hall.

"You didn't know your way to the bedroom, and I thought...I thought...I would show you the way. Good Lord, Kes, you're naked. And beautiful. Beautiful naked." Drew removed the candle from her hand and placed it on a nearby windowsill.

"Shouldn't I be naked?" she had enough time to ask before Drew pulled her into his arms and his mouth sealed hers in a kiss of monumental proportions.

Another hall, she mused. They seemed to have an affinity for narrow passages that connected rooms. Nothing in life was an accident. So what did their always making-out in a hallway mean?

And then Kesley couldn't think anymore, never mind analyze. Maintaining her balance took all her focus. Soon, even standing upright proved beyond her. She felt so woozy.

Drew, intuiting her dilemma, swept her up into his arms and carried her, presumably to his room, his kisses so full of raw power it was like riding the eye of a storm. Rather than pull back, rather than try to protect herself from the savagery of his kisses, she pulled his head down closer to hers, meeting his tongue with her own, eagerly running the tip over his teeth, the roof of his mouth, and everything in between.

Gasping for air, she came up for a quick breath. "Oh, dear."

He whispered against the corner of her mouth. "Are you sure you want this?"

No needed to collect herself before answering that question. "Yes." She stroked his cheek. "Yes."

"Damn," he muttered. "No light. Be right back."

After installing the forgotten candle on the nightstand, he placed her in the new bed, all made up, canopy in place.

"May I touch you?" His arms hung rigidly at his sides.

"Yes. Why are you waiting?"

He made a hoarse sound, knelt on the bed, and then he was cupping a breast, the point of her nipple poking the center of his palm. His enclosing fingers felt unlike anything she had ever felt before, his tenderness unexpected.

Or maybe not. When had Drew's touch ever been anything less than tender? When had he not given her his full consideration?

The unexpectedness came from her perceptions—or misconceptions. She had pegged Drew as an entirely unconventional man, and yet here they were in this lovely home in a neighborhood that would rival any peaceful oasis in suburbia, in a bedroom furnished with Williamsburg reproduction pieces. It didn't get more traditional than that. Maybe she needed to revise her expectations of Drew. Maybe she had him locked in a place he'd already left, only she hadn't taken the time to notice. She was moving on. Evidently, so was Drew. Without her.

"Your breasts are perfect." His thumb pressed the center of one. "So round and pretty. I noticed them the first day we met. I didn't want to stare. Didn't want you to think I was a creep."

"You noticed my breasts the day we met?"

"Oh, yeah," he answered, fondling the aforementioned, thumbs flicking across the hardened tips. "You were wearing a flowing peasant blouse thing. It was white, with flowers at the neckline you had embroidered yourself, and I could make out your nipples under your bra. In your innocence, you didn't know that I could, that any man could. You were so nice and friendly, talking a mile a minute, and I felt bad for noticing. I quick dropped my eyes to the floor. But to do that, my gaze had to move past your crotch, and that set me wondering about your pussy. The jeans you had on were tight, you see, and I could make out the slight hollow. You kept gabbing about your courses, telling me you wanted to work with troubled kids, and here you were little older than a kid yourself."

"You're only six months older than me."

"In life experience, I was years older than you, sweetheart. We come from two different places. I knew that, you didn't. Your thing was to help troubled teens and I admired you so much for that because my thing was to make a bundle of money."

"By the looks of *things*, you succeeded."

"Yeah, I did. So did you. We both got what we wanted, though they were two different things." His hand smoothed its way to her belly. "So sweet, and no clue to what I was thinking. So I turned away. I forget the excuse I used. But you tugged on my shirtsleeve and asked what was wrong in that direct way of yours. And what was I supposed to answer, sweetheart? Was I supposed to say, my brain was all wrapped up in your cunt? Was I supposed to tell you I wanted to fuck you? You would have been outraged. With good cause. You didn't understand where my mind was at. You still don't."

"Then tell me, Drew. Tell me what you're thinking."

He shook his head. "I'd rather show you." He lounged on the bed, and his hand, now on her pubic curls, started combing. "So soft. So sweet. I've never known anyone as soft and sweet as you, Kes. I didn't know there were girls like you in the world." A finger split the lips of her sex. "You're wet, sweetheart."

"I feel wet."

"Wet or not, sex will hurt the first time."

"I'm glad it will be you." She pressed his hand deeper into her vagina.

"No further," he said, his thumb finding her clitoris, delicately rubbing. "Feel good?"

She didn't close her eyes. "Yes."

"I'll be gentle."

"You don't have to tell me that. I already know." Her hand tunneled inside his shirt. "Your heart is going about a hundred miles an hour."

"Because I'm terrified."

Her lips feathered his throat with kisses. "There's no need for terror."

"Easy for you to say. You're only losing a scrap of flesh. I might be losing a whole person."

Chapter Sixteen

Drew undressed beside the bed, his eyes never leaving his sweetheart's beautiful face, candlelit in the otherwise darkened room. As he pulled on a rubber, done too many times before to count, he went over his strategy once more.

The best thing to do, he had decided last night when he couldn't sleep, was to get in and get out fast. Storm the gates and break the barrier. If she wasn't in mortal agony, he'd give her a few gentle pumps, just to satisfy her curiosity, and then get the hell out of there. He didn't intend to get off, but he was determined she'd get hers—accomplished manually. Clit stimulation after a shallow and brief penetration was the way to go. Right after she climaxed, while her body was still boneless with release, he'd hold her and kiss her to sleep in his arms.

Keeping to his side of the bed, Drew took her lips. Apprehensive about what was to come, all his thoughts concentrated on just getting through the ordeal that loomed ahead, he resigned himself to enjoying the sex about as much as he would with a vinyl blow-up doll.

The thing was, though, Kes was so damn good at kissing. So amazingly good at kissing that, despite his trepidation, he started losing himself to her mouth opening under his, her lips clinging, her tongue playfully engaging his in a mating dance. Her arms had twined themselves around his neck and her fingers were doing these sexy things, these hot, sexy things, to the back of his neck, and hell, that spot was no erogenous zone, but it sure felt like one now.

When her arched back caused her ribs to lift, her round breasts rose too, the nipples jutting like two succulent berries, Drew forgot his virgin nervousness. Yeah, he was a virgin too—to making love.

He broke the kiss to suck in air, his growing excitement turning his normally smooth, breast-cupping technique into a clumsy fumble. He'd meant to gently cup her, but his uncoordinated fingers moved on her nipples like clamps. He was groping her in jerky, grabby, pulling motions, like a novice, like a green kid who didn't know his way around a tit.

She gasped.

"Sorry," he rasped. "Sorry. I don't know what's happening. Did I hurt you? I never want to hurt you."

"Harder, harder, Drew. Do it harder."

Huh?

Harder? She wanted him to do her harder?

Somehow, he rolled on top of her, and his mouth found her nipple. His well-laid plans flew out the window, and he sucked that nipple like it was candy, dragging the elongated nub into his mouth with his teeth, just about swallowing her whole.

"Yes, yes, yes," she screamed, her leg coming up and over him, her foot on his spine, her hand going between her belly and his belly, her palm rolling his balls.

"Oh Christ, oh Christ," he whimpered, her nipple popping out of his mouth.

He reared up higher, over her higher, mounting her higher. He had yet to stroke her clit, because she was doing this really terrific trick with her hand on his cock, ringing it, forcing the blood to swell. Oh, man, where had she learned that trick?

Concentrate! He had to concentrate. This was for Kes, not for him. *Stroke her clit, fool!*

Drew reached between their bodies.

Her pubic curls were so soft, so incredibly soft, her pussy lips so moist, her cunt so open...

Concentrate!

His finger found the trigger. Pressed. Tenderly. Unselfishly. Prepared to work it 'til his hand went numb. Kes was a virgin. This could take hours.

One flick, and she let out a high-pitched scream, her pleasured cry rocking his world.

Yanking him deeper between her legs, she snapped, "Get in here," and slapped his ass.

He nearly came right then. "Wait, sweetheart, wait."

"*You* wait. I'm ready."

She was, and his control joined his plans, both flown out the window.

His hardness, his cock, his greedy dick, nudged the notch, the condom-covered head persuasively penetrating the threshold of her heat. Lifting up to meet him, rubber-sheathed-steel to silky-wet flesh, intrusion to acceptance, trespass to welcome, her body took him inside.

Not deep enough. Not nearly deep enough.

"Aw, sweetheart," he moaned and pressed inwards. "Hold onto my hands. Don't let go."

He pushed, piercing the barrier with one clean thrust, tasting her cry in his mouth, their fingers locked together.

"You okay?" he found the courage to ask.

"That was it? It's gone?"

"Yeah, it's history. The worst is over."

In the candlelit room she grinned. "Get cracking and show me the best."

He filled her. All of him, all of her. One person now. A gentle rocking of his hips, and they were on their way.

His kiss moved to the outer edge of her mouth so they could still talk. "That's right," he whispered. "Like that." His tongue came out and licked her bottom lip. "I can feel you, sweetheart. You're wrapped all around me. Warm.

Tight and snug. You're my shelter, Kes. You've always been my safe shelter. Tell me I can stay?"

"I want you to stay. I want you to show me, Drew. Show me everything."

"I will. You just tell me when."

"Now," she cried. "Show me now."

He proceeded to do just that.

Chapter Seventeen

Kesley felt Drew's penis swell within her, the pace of his strokes quickening from slow to fast to frantic. He had begun to surge, his thrusts much too frenzied for her to match.

She tried anyway. Using her newfound internal muscles, she squeezed him as he stroked her, mimicking his every move. The mutuality only seemed to spur him on, his powerful strokes increasing in intensity. He drove up into her, his male strength, his beat, his rhythm, his fast dance beautiful to behold.

Orgasm. Climax. Coming. That precipice of pleasure, that edge of sensation encroached, almost within reach.

"Can't...can't...can't slow it down. It's too much," Drew growled, sweating, shaking, his muscles gone rigid.

Kesley knew without knowing that Drew was about to ejaculate.

Too soon for her. She wouldn't scale the pinnacle, not this time. It wouldn't happen for her this time. Not this time.

She held onto his heaving shoulders, his flesh slippery with perspiration, his muscles clenched, felt him struggle against the cataclysm of upheaval, felt him lose the struggle.

His body strained. Bucked. Went taut. "Sorry, sorry, sorry, sweetheart," he groaned. With one last thrust up into her body, her lover came on a deep-throated grunt.

Drew stilled for all of thirty seconds, before pulling out.

"Are you okay?" he asked, throwing himself off her. "Did I hurt you? I didn't know how else to do it. I suspected maybe quick was better and..."

"I'm fine, Drew." With a cat-like stretch, she smiled, remarkably pleased with herself, at knowing she had pleased him. "Absolutely fine. And now that the messy deflowering has been accomplished we can get down to the fun part."

His gaze dipped to her thighs. "You're bleeding. Christ, I'm sorry."

"Would you stop apologizing? A little blood is to be expected."

"But a man looks down and sees blood on the woman he just made love to and all kinds of stuff goes through his head. Complicated stuff. I feel like I hurt you and yet I'm proud too that I was the first you allowed into your body, that you gave me your virginity. It was a gift. Still, the violence of cutting through your flesh..."

He shook his head. "It's weird...I feel like one of those Vikings of old who went around ravishing virgins."

"Give me a few minutes to catch my breath and feel free to ravish me again."

He looked down into her eyes. "No fooling around, Kes. This is too important not to take seriously."

"I am serious. I do want you to ravish me again."

"You've gotta know this—I have never ravished a woman. I have never done anything with a woman that wasn't consensual and the women I did those consensual things with were as experienced as me in fun and games. And that's all it ever was, fun and games."

As she tried to figure out why Drew was telling her all this now, he left the bed. Without turning his back to her, he rolled off the condom, dropping the semen-filled reservoir in a plastic-lined wastebasket. Obviously, he had prepared in advance.

Though the activity was more about housekeeping than romance, her already hardened nipples tingled in arousal. She never would have suspected that she would find cleaning up after sex so erotic, but she did. It was the intimacy involved, she realized. The fact he hadn't turned away, though his penis was now flaccid and much smaller than when he had removed his clothes. That Drew trusted her with that visual information, that he had freely allowed her to see him at his most vulnerable, warmed her heart. And other places too.

Propping her arms behind her head, better to enjoy the sight of that smaller, slightly wilted-looking penis, her smile widened.

There were distinct advantages to losing one's virginity to—or, for that matter, going to bed for the first time with—a man one knows you through and through. Because she trusted Drew as much as he trusted her, she experienced not a twinge of first-time-sex embarrassment. She had thoroughly enjoyed—no, that was too tame a description—she had been thoroughly blown away by everything, all of it, every earthy detail of being with him. She couldn't have chosen a better candidate to deflower her than the prime masculine specimen before her. Gorgeous to look at and well-hung, even when deflated. Drew was also a darling, a considerate and caring lover. He had so much tenderness inside him. So much kindness. What more could a girl ask for?

Suddenly excruciatingly aware of that most private part of her body, that new consciousness heightening her sex drive, she conceded that she *could* indeed ask for more. And another go round with this gorgeous well-hung specimen would be her first request.

Understatement. If she didn't have him again, she'd die. Now to convince him of the same.

Tough to do considering he had just rushed from the room.

He returned carrying a facecloth and a towel.

Knowing instinctively what they were for, she reached for them.

"No. Let me," Drew said softly. He sat down next to her on the bed and proceeded to care for her. Or rather, make that, *take care of her*. She wasn't completely dense—she knew Drew already cared for her. As a friend. But now that they'd had sex, his caring for her had taken on a new meaning, a deeper meaning.

As he bathed the proof of her virginity from the inside of her thighs, then delicately cleansed the bloodstained folds of her pussy—the cold compress infinitely soothed—she grew hot and restless.

Deeper meaning be damned Plain and simple, his careful strokes were turning her on. *Drew* turned her on.

"You're swollen," he said softly, gazing between her legs with an intensity that stirred her even more. After patting her dry with the towel, he touched her. One digit. Lightly. A butterfly caress. "So pretty," he whispered, looking up into her eyes. "You're pretty all over, sweetheart."

Then, her attentive but maddening lover jumped off the bed. Again.

She knew why. Drew didn't want to hurt her.

Bosh!

She wanted to do it all. In particular, she wanted IT to happen.

Orgasm. Coming. Release. That was what this exercise was all about. And she'd gotten close. She had tottered on the brink. The chasm was within a few strokes. Drew could push her over the edge. All he had to do was stop being so damn considerate.

In a fever of sexual excitement, Kesley freed a hand from behind her head and brought it to her pussy. Little point in modesty now. She stretched a leg out wide and bent the knee up high. In full view of Drew, who had just audibly gulped. Good.

"Mmm," she murmured a finger ringing her vaginal opening. The action combined with the heated utterance placed her lover's attention exactly where she wanted it.

"Mmm," she murmured again, the tip of her finger slipping inside.

She had been wet from the lube on the condom, wet from a trickle of blood, wet from her own excitement.

She had not been wet with Drew's semen.

And she felt the loss. She wanted to be wet with Drew's ejaculate, to be sticky with his cum, to know in the most basic of ways that she had belonged to him, their body fluids merging.

"Christ," he groaned, following the direction of her hand, watching as her finger dipped into her vulva, probing the only very slightly swollen lips.

She eyed the jut of Drew's penis. The sight of her masturbating had excited him.

"Mmm," she murmured with another sultry stretch. "I need you, Drew."

"What you need is to wait. Rome wasn't built in a day ya know."

She didn't need a travelogue. She needed Drew's fine cock pounding up inside her, deep inside, reaching her where she needed to be reached. He could dissolve the knot of frustration in her belly. She could fly with Drew. And after ten years of knowing him, she could read his expression. Waiting was not what he wanted either. He wanted to be inside her again as much as she wanted him there.

He took a step back toward the bed, his features hardening along with his cock, his eyes glinting on her opening. "I can usually last hours without going off. I couldn't that time."

"Sorry. Guess it's me."

He stretched out on the bed beside her again, not touching her, a muscled arm flung over his eyes. So he couldn't look? Or, so she wouldn't see how much she affected him?

"Yeah, it's you," he said hoarsely. "And there's no reason to say you're sorry. I knew doing it with you would be different, but I didn't know how different. Let me tell you a secret. There are mind tricks I use to keep going. I know every one of 'em will fail with you. You slay me, Kes. Positively slay me. I'm dying here, sweetheart, inch by inch." Removing his arm, he turned and looked at her.

She arched her back, played with a peaked nipple, the other hand still moving between her legs. "Yes, it was very nice, wasn't it?"

"*Nice?* You call what we just did fuckin' nice? I'm flattened."

"Oh, dear. I hope that won't alter your agreement to act as my sex surrogate. I'll need you to penetrate me multiple times, and in every position. Then there are the refinements. The addendums. Most men expect a BJ, and I'll have to practice to get it down right."

"At a moment like this—how can you be so glib?"

"Because I'm committed to this. I need a man in my life, sexually. And I need a relationship that will lead to marriage and children. I intend to excel at sex, Drew."

"Always the over-achiever," he said with a sigh.

"Well, will you help me get what I want?"

He looked away. "We both need time to regroup, Kes."

That's what he *said,* but once again, she could tell he was ready to go. Chivalrous Drew. She intended to wear him down. Once her mind was set, she never gave up. Didn't he know that about her? "In that case, I guess I'll go take a shower. Want to be the first man I've ever showered with? I think that pulsating head on the nozzle would alleviate some of the soreness. What do you think?"

No longer looking away, Drew eyed her elongated nipples now, his heavy gaze trailing to the center of her body, to her pussy. "Yeah. Okay. A shower." He grabbed the candle.

She rose from the bed. With a wiggle in her step that had never been present before, Kesley headed for the shower. Drew followed, his gaze so hot on her swaying bottom she actually felt his eyes brand her skin.

"I'm thinking about getting a tattoo on my butt," she flung over her shoulder. "Do men find them sexy?"

"You're not getting a tattoo."

"That's not what I asked."

"You're not getting a tattoo, Kes."

"If the man in my life wants me tattooed, I will get a tattoo. The same goes for piercing. I'd get a nipple or my pussy, or both done, for the guy in my life. I intend to be very compliant with my lover or lovers. I think I have the makings of a submissive. I think I have the natural inclination to allow a man to dominate me in the bedroom. What do you think, Drew? Do submissive women do it for you?"

"You do it for me. And you're not getting pierced or tattooed."

In the hallway on the way to the bathroom, he pulled her to a halt. "Understand?"

What she understood was that her lover was aroused, and more dominant than she'd given him credit for. Who knew he'd be the take-charge type? She'd only been teasing about the piercing and the tattoo, only joking about her submissive bend, only to have inadvertently stumbled upon a latent authoritarian streak in the ordinarily laid-back Drew. This titillating turn of events pleased her enormously, as did his enormous cock. And what was it about hallways, anyway? Here they were back in one again—

His free hand fell on her bottom cheek. "You have a killer ass, sweetheart. And I won't stand for you marking it."

"Okay, Drew, while we're together, I promise, no tattoos. After that, you lose the right to an opinion. You'll have no authority over my ass then."

He pushed her to the wall. "Open your legs."

She did immediately, without question, and his hand moved between her thighs to her pubic hair.

"No strange guy in some tattoo parlor or a piercing salon is putting their hands on you, especially not where my hand is now. You're not getting naked and spreading your legs for a piercing, you're not having your skin shot with dye. Your silky flesh is not getting inked." Leaning into her, he turned her jaw towards him and kissed her hard and deep. But when his penis nudged her, he pulled back.

"Don't go," she whispered. Taking a step forward, she wiggled her hips enticingly.

"Cut it out." Reaching around behind her, he smacked her bare bottom, and not at all gently. A harbinger of things to come?

Oh, she hoped so And it suddenly occurred to Kesley that Drew's masterful qualities shouldn't have surprised her. After all, he was a successful entrepreneur, powerful in his own sphere of expertise. He'd started his consulting business from scratch. With no help from anyone, he had built his company from the ground up. He had always made light of his accomplishments, never bragging or even accepting full credit, always pointing to his employees rather than himself for his success. But achieving what he'd achieved had taken a tremendous amount of ambition and drive. Also, despite his chronic slouch, Drew was physically strong. The guy had muscles on top of muscles—just because he didn't flaunt them didn't mean they weren't there.

Drew, she decided, only showed her the funny and nurturing parts of himself. What other traits had he kept hidden all these years?

She purred in anticipation of finding out.

"Get in the shower, Kes. If you're into compliance, I'll give you plenty to comply with later, and that's a promise."

In the bathroom, she stepped into the stall. After setting down the candle and turning on the water, Drew got in too, taking up a position directly behind her.

In the steamy enclosure, he washed her. Not with the neatly folded square of terry on the soap dish. With his lathered hands. Everywhere. When he told her to lift her arms or open her thighs, she did. When he lifted her breasts and massaged each with foamy rose-scented bubbles, she abandoned herself to his ministrations. When his hand moved to her bottom and washed her there, she said not a word. Even when he opened her up in back, and soaped between her cheeks, his fingers moving deep within the crevice, slowly within the crevice, thoroughly within the crevice, she offered no resistance. In fact, the naughtiness of it all thrilled her.

Extending a hand, he removed the shower massage and rinsed her. "Let's see if this helps ease your pussy," he said. "Open up."

She split her legs.

"No, with your hand. Open your pussy up with your hand."

With two fingers, she pulled up on the folds.

Still standing behind her, he sent the pulsating spray into her vagina.

Her jaw lifted, her head fell back against his chest and she groaned into the humid air as Drew sprayed shot after shot of gently vibrating water upwards into her very open vagina.

"Feel good?" he asked, his free hand kneading a breast.

Her mouth opened to speak, but no words came out. Convulsively swallowing, she settled for a nod.

Drew returned the showerhead back where it belonged.

She knew the exact moment when he took his penis in hand. In the beginning, when he had washed her, his penis had merely bumped against her. Now he purposefully directed the hardened head. The thick blunt tip prodded her back to front, then shallowly entered her back to front, then rubbed into her back to front, an incrementally deepening penetration.

"Bend over," he growled.

Bracing her arms against the wall, she rounded her spine and lifted her hips for him as his penis pushed across her slit.

"You make it easy for a man," he rasped.

"I am making it easy for *you*," she qualified.

"Really?" he said, kissing her nape. "That enthusiastic?"

"I want it all, Drew. Every experience. The way I see it, I have a lot of catching up to do. Almost thirty is a little late for losing one's virginity. I'm coming from behind."

"Me too." He gave a lecherous chuckle.

Appetite whetted, she hinted for more. "I'm not opposed to any position."

"Glad to hear it. I'll file your lack of opposition away. For another time. My cock isn't going in any more tonight."

"No?" she said, looking over her shoulder. It looked and felt like his cock was going in to her.

"No. I already got mine, but you didn't get yours. That makes me less than a gentleman. So, my fortunate little sweetheart, you're getting my tongue." He ran a finger down her rounded spine. "You can straighten up now."

When she had, he shut off the water, and helped her exit the stall just like a gentleman. Drew had always shown her every politeness a man can show a woman, from opening doors to carrying bundles, and his dominance in no way diluted his consideration.

As she stood naked and aroused on the bath rug, he applied a towel to her hair and briskly rubbed. "First, though, before you get my tongue, I'm drying you off."

"Highly unlikely. I don't think I can get any wetter," she wisecracked as he applied the towel to her breasts.

The rough toweling making her crazy, her skin glowing pink from his attention, she flushed all over with sexual heat.

Her tormentor put the towel aside and dropped to his knees at her feet. Carefully rubbing his cheeks back and forth against her belly—surely done so as not to abrade her skin—he fingered, then circled, and then delicately separated the outer lips of her sex. He breathed lustfully across the opening.

Gasping, she pressed his blond head, the hair darkened to gold because of the shower, against her. "If you're trying to blow me dry, forget it. That activity will not accomplish your goal."

With a chuckle, he blew on her pussy again, the warm puff of breath bringing on the shivers. "Drew, please?" she begged, all playfulness gone from her voice. "I can't take much more."

He looked up at her. "Let's get you back to bed."

"I want it to happen with you inside me. With your penis inside me."

He bit her knee, and then her thigh. She trembled from head to foot. "It will."

"Are you so sure?" she asked, suddenly not as sure. "Some women work their whole sexual careers to achieve climax and never succeed."

"You'll have one with me inside you," he promised. "And there won't be any work involved, just enjoyment. And you better not discuss any of this during your bitch-and-cry group. Some things are not open to discussion, like my talented tongue for instance." That talented tongue darted into her bellybutton and she yelped, crying out when his mouth opened over her belly.

She had a tummy. She hated sit-ups, and no matter how many miles she logged in jogging, her round little pot wouldn't go away. Drew's abs were deliciously flat, and he did nothing at all to earn them. He had received many gifts at birth, and because of those gifts, women fell into his arms with ridiculous ease. Was he comparing her to any of them?

"I love your body, Kes," he said, sucking on her unflat tummy. "I love everything about it. Here on out, I plan on keeping you naked."

An impossibility. She had a job to return to bright and early the next morning, and a love bite on her plump belly was no reason to call in sick. "Who needs a tattoo when I can have a hickey," she panted.

"The first of many," he replied and picked her up in his arms. He carried her back to the bed, dropping her into the middle of the mattress where she bounced, legs and arms akimbo. Diving in after her, his hands split her thighs, spreading her wide. A heel of a foot in each hand, his mouth landing where she needed him the most, he blew and kissed and lapped at her thighs, before his tongue entered the folds with a short jab.

He let go of her feet and she bucked on the bed. Like a wild thing, she screamed and tore her fingers through his hair. Pulled, yanked, nearly scalped him as he went at her with gusto, his tongue piercing her center over and over again. With his skull squeezed between her legs, she came on a sob.

Afterwards, he kissed his way up her body, from the small knoll of her belly to the valley of her cleavage.

"In the name of advancing your education," he said, plundering her mouth in much the same way he had plundered between her legs, giving her a pussy-flavored kiss before his mouth descended again. The valley. The knoll. The pussy. His talented tongue slipping inside.

After another buck, scream and sob, she waited impatiently while he traveled back up her body again.

He smiled down into her face. "Christ, Kes, you're like a keg of dynamite."

"I seem to have all the signs of sex addiction," she replied happily, high on the drug of him. "Unfortunately, that fix will need to do me 'til next we meet."

"Next we meet?" He sat up. "What does that mean? Where are you going?"

She swung her legs over the edge of the bed. "Home."

"What ever happened to us sleeping together?"

"We just did."

"No, I mean as in snoring."

"I would like to. There are the elbows etcetera I need to get used to in bed. But, alas, I have decided to implement a strict rule against spending the night with a lover. This does not preclude the occasional post-coital nap."

"What? For the sake of some dumb-ass arbitrary rule, you're leaving me to rattle around in this big house alone, in this big bed, my first night here?"

"You never spend the night with a lover, do you?" She sent him a probing look. "Well, *do* you?"

"I told you I never do."

"So why should I? What's good for the teacher is good for the student."

She went to the bathroom, and came back out carrying her pile of clothes. "People learn by example," she said, finding her underwear in the rolled up ball.

"Yeah, they do, Kes. But they don't always continue to follow a bad example set for them by someone else. People can change," he grumbled. "By the way, speaking of changing—no bra. No panties. You won't need them in the SUV."

"Oh, but I'm not accepting a ride home from you. I'm taking a cab."

"I just took your virginity. I'm driving you home."

"As I begin, so too shall I proceed. After leaving a lover's bed, I cab it home. Unless, of course, I live with the man in a committed relationship and then we'll already be home, in which case we can snuggle for the rest of the night in our very own bed."

"I-want-to-drive-you-home," he shouted, obviously in a foul mood, a rare occurrence for the affable Drew.

Had she struck a nerve? Would he now commit to something—if only an insight into his past motivations and his future plans? Would he risk giving her more than his body? Would he share what he was all about? She knew damn well he was about more than sexing it up with a bunch of one-night stand bimbos!

"Now don't get angry," she placated. "I'm only thinking of poor Mrs. Harris and her weak heart. If she sees a steady stream of strange men pulling up to the house she'll freak."

"What steady stream of strange men? I'm only one man, and Mrs. Harris knows me," he blustered.

Time to set him straight. Time to issue him a non-threatening ultimatum. *Get your ass in gear, Drew, and start spilling* "Remember that mile-wide swath you told me I'd be able to cut through all the eligible men in Boston?"

"Yeah, I remember. What of it?"

"Well, if Ted doesn't work out, I have a lot of swath-cutting to do," she said breezily. "A steady stream of swath cutting. That's why I'm cabbing it home. I'm only thinking of dear Mrs. Harris' health. At her advanced age, I don't think she'd appreciate the amount of men a girl has to sleep with to find Mr. Right." Kesley shook her head. "We could be talking thousands here. I do tend towards fussiness."

Drew gave her nothing, and so sparing him not a glance, Kesley climbed into her wrinkled clothes. After a brief search of her sling bag for her cell phone, she dialed the taxi.

She was no enabler

Chapter Eighteen

Kesley stood before her mail cubby at The Shelter, prioritizing envelopes, when someone tapped her shoulder.

She turned.

Doris handed her a manila folder. "The final report from the Med Van on John Smith," she explained.

"Thanks, Doris. I've been waiting for this, Kesley exclaimed. "How'd you end up with it?"

"For some reason, the Med Unit listed John Smith's case as still unassigned."

"Unassigned? When I've been calling over there twice a day looking for this additional dental information?" Kesley blew a breath up into her lank, too long bangs and then flipped open the cover sheet. And there it was on the computer readout in reassuring black and white numbers and graphs. In every respect, including dental, John was a normal and healthy teen.

Doris nudged her again. "He's waiting for you in your office."

"Who?" Kesley said distractedly, frowning at the slight number inside the weight category box.

"John Smith. Reception sent him on ahead per your prior approval." Doris' look held concern. "I hope you don't keep anything valuable at your desk, anything he can sell on the street for drugs."

"He's not a thief," Kesley said, and hurried away for her office.

As John was twenty pounds underweight for his lanky six-foot frame, the first order of business was to convince him to drop by for breakfast and lunch. Free food was a draw for any growing teen, particularly motivating for a homeless one. The Shelter's huge dining room also provided an excellent non-threatening gathering place where isolated kids could socialize.

Kesley stopped outside her open office door and peeked.

Inside, a young man sprawled on the chair next to her desk. Once again, and out of the blue, a vague and discomforting sense of familiarity struck her. John Smith reminded her of someone.

Who?

After a few seconds of concentrated effort—had she bumped into John inside a store, on the subway, bumming for spare change on Boston Commons?—she finally gave up pursuing the slippery memory. With an intentional warning rattle of the doorknob, she stepped into her office.

"Hi, John." She held up the folder in her hand. "Your medical report. According to this, apart from needing some dental work—three cavities in need of filling—you're a healthy specimen."

The runaway gave her a seldom seen smile. "Damn. I knew I should've been flossing more."

"You know what would ensure your continued good health?"

He folded his arms over his chest. "Drinking eight glasses of water a day and eating plenty of fiber?"

"We'll get to your diet in a minute. Right now, I'm thinking a work training program here at The Shelter."

"A hardcore case like me giving up my profession?"

She shook her head. "A profession is an occupation that requires considerable training and/or specialized study. A person involved in a profession makes an active choice to dedicate himself to the pursuit of learning his skill. That definition doesn't apply to what you do."

"I don't know about that—"

Louisa Trent

She interrupted. "You do what you do to scrape by. You're a smart kid, John, with a good brain. Use it!"

John's face turned to stone. She'd pushed too hard and, as a result, she was losing him. A change of subject was in order.

"The docs say in your medical report that you need to gain weight. How's about you start showing up here every morning for breakfast? Green does the cooking." A blatant bribe to get him in the door.

John's tight expression loosened. "She does?"

"Yep. And the lady cooks a mean scrambled egg."

"I can't."

She pressed. "Why not?"

"I work nights, remember? So I oversleep most mornings."

An excuse. A defense against getting too close to Green of the soft eyes and caring heart. John feared that girl, because he liked her. Enough to stick around?

John reclaimed his feet. "Listen, nice chatting with you and all that, Miss Richmond, but I really gotta go. Business, you know?"

And with that, the runaway ran away.

Kesley sat at her desk staring at two flies on the wall, an overwhelming sense of defeat immobilizing her.

After five minutes of virtual paralysis, she left her office. Walking down the hall, she stopped at the receptionist's desk.

"If anyone asks, Bernie, I'm taking my lunch break early. Back in forty-five minutes. An hour, tops."

Refusing to give up without a fight, Kesley skipped lunch and went out looking for a watch—with an alarm feature. Nothing elaborate, nothing a street kid would hawk for drugs. Tomorrow night was Thursday, and once again, she would canvass the teen hangouts with the street-workers. She'd steer them to the park where John "worked" and give him the watch. Something as simple as a buzzer sounding every morning at the same time served as an effective first step in transitioning a kid back into the mainstream.

A sense of time helped to normalize a disenfranchised kid, gave a sense of order and importance and priority to what might otherwise be long, aimless days. After John started showing up for meals, she'd get him interested in some low-stress, low-structured programs, either recreational or skill building activities. A schedule created order out of chaos, provided a sense of security, gave a kid a reason to move forward.

But even as she made plans, Kesley had a sinking feeling John would never move forward until he allowed himself to look back.

◆ ◆ ◆

Kesley had pulled another all-nighter on Wednesday. On Thursday, a twenty-four hour shift kept her away from him. It was now early Friday evening, and Drew hadn't seen his girl in almost seventy-two hours. Some sex explosion they were having.

When he called her at work, just to hear the sound of her voice, just to find out how she was doing, just to keep from going crazy without her, she informed him in so many words that they'd have to put their lust marathon on hold.

What the hell was going on with her and this new runaway case?

She refused talk to him about it, but tension crackled in her voice. Drew's gut told him Kes feared losing the kid she had been desperately trying to bring in from the streets. And when that happened, she always took it hard, like it was a personal failure or something.

Drew knew different. A non-cooperative kid wasn't a failure. Not hers. Not anyone's. Sometimes people, young and old and in-between, just weren't ready to make a change in their lives. A kid uncooperative in the present could always turn his situation around in the future.

Or maybe not.

Sometimes a young male needed to hit rock bottom first before putting forth the effort required to make something out of nothing. When a person sinks to the lowest point, previously unwelcome options start getting some serious exploration. When a kid finally realizes he's drowning in the sludge of his own go-nowhere life, he's more apt to reach out to an extended hand, to accept the lifesaver offered him.

Leastwise, that's how Drew remembered it. Looking back on his early years, that was how it had happened for him.

At eighteen, he'd been on the streets, panhandling spare change, doing some other stuff, too, to survive, stuff he'd just as soon not think about now. He'd been going down for the third count, drowning in his own self-hatred, when he entered a program similar to the one offered at The Shelter. There, he had gotten his act together and his life in control and his attitude adjusted.

Kes didn't know that about him, and Drew was keeping it quiet. His past was in the past and that's where he wanted it kept. Whenever he had the opportunity, he gave back in his own way, helping troubled kids through mentoring whenever he could, making financial donations, and let it go at that. His lost years were staying lost. He would never open them up to general conversation. Some things in a man ran too deep to discuss.

Kes had to be the bravest, toughest, strongest person he'd ever met. But even she needed a shoulder to cry on when things turned to shit. Why was she closing down on him?

Not letting him in hurt real bad. Why had she turned the key and locked him out? Regardless of their no-shop-talk agreement, she could still discuss this kid. Open up to him. Get what was bothering her off her chest.

He'd broach the subject while they were jogging. Whenever he was home from his travels, especially on the weekends, they always made a point of running around Jamaica Pond together. During their special time, they'd catch up on what was happening in one another's lives, generally shoot the bull, be there for one another. Why should that change just because they'd done the deed?

The deed.

That's what he used to call it. Not any more. He'd made love to Kes. Afterwards, he had wanted to hold her. Sleep with her in his arms. What did he care about an antique bed? For fuck's sake, he'd slept in alleyways, in dumpsters, in stranger's bedrooms—he didn't give two shits about heirloom furniture. He'd bought the bed for Kes, because she liked nice things, meaningful things, and then she hadn't wanted to sleep with him. Why hadn't she wanted to spend the night with him?

Kes was real big on rules, but not sleeping with a date was some stupid rule, as it applied to him—he wasn't just any date He was the man who loved her. Had always loved her. Why couldn't she open up her big pretty eyes and see that?

Maybe because he couldn't tell her he loved her. Not yet. He couldn't rush her, not in the place where her head was at. Right now, she was all about spreading her sexual wings. He understood. So he'd give her some time, then reveal he worshipped the ground she walked on—

Before Kes did any of that bogus mile-wide swath-cutting.

She wasn't the one-night stand type. And he wasn't about to let her, anyway. Did she really believe he would stand back while she walked out of his life? If she thought that about him, she didn't know him very well—

He couldn't blame her on that score. His own fault that she misunderstood his motivations. After all, he had never given her the chance to really know him, to know where he'd been and understand where he still wanted to go.

He had plans. Big plans. And they included her. Only he hadn't told her about his past, so he couldn't tell her about his plans for the future either.

That might have to change. If telling meant the difference between keeping and losing her, he might have to peel back the skin and show her the scars that didn't show on the outside. Whatever keeping her took, that's what he would do to hang onto Kes.

Back at the three-decker, after giving a big friendly wave to Mrs. Harris on ground zero, Drew took the stairs. At the top landing, he stopped, and faced the door.

Okay, now what was he supposed to do? The door stumped him. Should he turn the knob and go in, just like always, or knock first and wait for her to get up from whatever she was doing and let him in?

His hand went to the knob. Why inconvenience her? She might be getting dressed for her jog. Damn inconsiderate to interrupt.

Damn inconsiderate to walk in on her too. It's not like he had any rights—

Wait a minute. He was her lover—hard to believe, as sleeping with her still felt like a dream to him—and that gave him some rights.

He'd worn a condom, figuring the reservoir at the tip would go unfilled. Once he'd made her virginity history, he figured a few gentle strokes and that would be that.

He figured wrong.

They say you can never go home again, and that saying applied to him one hundred percent. After making his escape at the age of thirteen from a foster kid placement that had never really been a home, he had never looked back. Being inside Kes felt like he had finally found a place where he belonged. Not wanting to burden her with all that messy crap, he hadn't told her that she was the closest he had ever gotten to having a home.

And then he'd gone and behaved unworthily.

That first time, he had gotten his, but she hadn't gotten anything but pain. How selfish could a guy get?

That first time, she had almost grabbed that spectacular brass ring. Maybe if he'd hung on a few strokes longer…

But he couldn't hang on, not without driving deep, not without causing her more pain. And then it was too late anyway. When he needed his control, her responsiveness shot it out from under him. The way she hugged him to her, like she didn't want to let him go, that was when he had lost his grip altogether and gone off like a cannon.

As soon as he'd finished, he'd wanted to start in all over again. Knowing she had to be sore, knowing she had to be hurting, still all he could think about was pushing them both to the limit. He'd called up all his willpower and yanked himself out, propelling himself to the edge of the mattress, where he had hunkered down, not touching her.

One touch and he would have turned into a plundering barbarian. So he'd kept his distance, shaking because he wanted to touch her so bad. Then, after saying she was okay—that was one huge load off—Kes did this sexy as all hell move and started talking about the "fun part".

Fun part? She wore a crimson stain on her body, a stain he had put there. He wasn't thinking fun. He was thinking dark stuff, stuff he didn't want to think.

She'd bled. The sight nearly strangled him with fear. He knew women bled the first time, but so much?

The sight of her virgin's blood had also excited him, made him feel possessive too, like he had just claimed her in the most primal of rites. When he stared into her compassionate eyes, he knew Kes was too innocent, too damn nice to understand what was going on in his mind. Some seriously dangerous stuff swirled around inside his head. They were getting into some areas where saints like Kesley should fear to tread.

He'd forced himself to leave the bed, intentionally taking care of business in front of her, ridding himself of the used rubber smeared with her blood. For sure, he had never done *that* in front of a woman before. So as not to break the romantic moment, afterwards, he always cleaned up in the bathroom.

With Kes, he needed real, and cleaning up after sex was as real as real got.

The honesty backfired. Under her watchful stare, he had started to get hard all over again. He never meant for it to happen. Too soon for it to happen. Usually, he took a while to get erect again. But there it was, a hard-on to end all hard-ons, a reality too large to be denied. And that was before she had started touching herself.

An unconscious gesture, he thought at first. Until a lusty "Mmm" escaped her slightly parted lips.

His innocent Kes had treated him to a hardcore peep show! His straight as an arrow sweetheart, a girl-next-door if ever there was one, had played to his man's fantasies, masturbating right in front of him, where he could see.

Unable to look away, his cock had just about launched at the sight of her pleasuring herself.

And what had she done?

The hussy had smiled at him. He had just about busted a nut, and there she was, grinning from ear to ear at him. Like making him lose control was a good thing. It was not a good thing. It was a very, very, bad thing when a man lost his control.

"Mmm." Her body had undulated—the witch.

He'd approached the bed, her pussy his destination, only to collapse next to her, his throat so dry with lust he could barely speak, an arm over his burning eyes, afraid to go near, unable to keep away. His cock had been on fire, sticking straight up, the head dripping pre-cum. Her right to see him for the man he was inside. Weak, unsure, scared.

And what did she say, the little cock-tease, after she'd stripped him of all his defenses, revealing all his manly insecurities, leaving him naked in his desire?

"Yes," said she, "it was very nice, wasn't it?"

"It" being that monumental, life-altering epiphany he'd just experienced.

Then, to add insult to injury, she'd told him she still planned on dating.

He was killing Ted, and any other creep who got near her.

Not comprehending the inherent dangers of a jealous man, Kes had continued to tease him, taunting him with piercings and tattooings, until he had felt like a bare wire looking for a socket to plug. She was wet, he was frayed. Conditions had been right for electrocution. Before they both got fried, he gave her seductive ass a warning spank.

The she-cat had meowed with pleasure.

In the shower stall, his soaped-up hands had moved all over her. Never, not even in his wildest wet dreams, had he ever pictured bathing with her. Bubbles and skin. Two slippery bodies. A man and a woman sighing. Erotic poetry.

In bed after the shower, Kes had come apart under his mouth, her honey dripping down his throat, her screams of release resounding in his ears, a man's finest praise from his woman.

So, now that they had passed from whatever they had been into something else, what was he supposed to do about private stuff, like closed apartment doors?

Drew lifted his hand, and knuckle-rapped the door. The echoing knock answered his unspoken question.

Until he worked up the courage to tell her the truth about his past, he had no rights over Kes.

Chapter Nineteen

As the sun went down over Jamaica Pond, the city heat dissipating with the encroachment of night, Kes began her usual round of warm-up exercises. She had weak ankles, and to prevent running injuries, the tendons required slow stretches.

This time, her restless mind just wasn't into it.

After only a few stretches, she started right in, running at a good clip.

Odd jogging alone. Odd, not to have Drew bullying her into a gradual buildup before her sprint. She missed his companionship, his sense of humor, his willingness to listen without interrupting. He never offered comments or suggestions when she talked about work. He never gave advice at all unless she came out and specifically asked. Even then, he knew that sometimes she just needed to vent.

Like about John Smith.

On Thursday night during outreach, she had found the teen runaway in the park, hustling in the same spot as before. During their subsequent conversation, she had handed over the wristwatch. He could not have pretended his delight over the gift. Dropping his cool routine, John had even agreed to start coming to The Shelter for breakfast.

"I like Green," he had bashfully confessed. "Breakfast will give me a good excuse to see her every day. Don't tell her I said so, 'kay, Miss Richmond?"

Naturally, Kesley had agreed.

John Smith had sounded so normal. Like any other young male with a crush on a girl, not wanting his secret given away to anyone, especially not to the object of his affections.

She would love to get Drew's take on him.

John, true to his word, had arrived right on time Friday morning for breakfast. And she had been deliriously happy to see him making friends with Green, and other kids too. Was he ready to begin a program? Or was she pushing too hard? Trying to make something happen too fast? Placing too much pressure on him? Was she putting her own personal timetable on John?

Was she doing the same with Drew?

She had purposefully forced change on them. After ten years together, they had reached a plateau of comfort that was both good and bad. Good, because they enjoyed one another's company. Bad, because since they had each other, they hadn't needed to reach out to anyone else. Drew had his one-night stands and she had no sex life whatsoever. They could have gone on like that for another decade, and that sort of co-dependency wasn't healthy. For either of them.

Sex had broken apart their safe little cocoon, forced them to relate to each other differently. But now that they had become physically intimate, what would happen to the emotional connection they'd always shared? Would a new pattern, a deeper pattern of relating to each other, develop? Or, would they fall by the wayside? Had Drew been right? Rather than strengthen their bond, would the introduction of sex cause the severance of their connection? Had that separation already started?

As Kesley's sneakers pounded the pavement, sadness ran at her back, dogging her heels, gaining momentum.

Looking out at the boats on the water, watching weekend sailors cram in those last few minutes of remaining daylight before night descended, she realized once again how easily people slipped out of one's life. Unless a concerted effort was made, and emotional ties were nurtured, even the strongest bonds grew weak, even the dearest people were cast off, left to drift away.

No one's fault. No one to blame. Losing track of people was simply a side effect of today's mobile world.

What would she ever do if she lost touch with Drew?

With all the demands placed on her time, on his time, something had to give. Would it be them? Former neighbors in the same three-decker—is that what they were destined to become? A stamp pressed on a Christmas card, a duty call on a birthday, a get-together maybe twice a year?

Caught up with their own separate and individual lives, even those overtures would peter out. Eventually, they would each of them join a cast of characters in the other's fleeting memories.

Huffing and puffing, Kesley finished circling the one-and-a-half mile pond. At the boathouse, as always, she felt an overwhelming urge to toss in the towel, usually in favor of a large chocolate-mocha ice cream cone.

Drew had never let her quit. He would deliberately pick some idiotic argument just to keep her going. Sometimes, he'd throw out some ridiculous dare so she'd compete with him. More often than not, though, he would just make her laugh. Clutching her side, sweat dripping off her skin, she'd forget about her fatigue, forget about throwing in the towel, and giggle her way around the pond again. Only to look over at her companion and stop laughing when she caught a glimpse of Drew looking blond and elegant and graceful, hardly breaking a sweat in his long-legged gait.

What she felt now, the urge to throw in the towel and quit—this was different. A crushing depression weighed her down. Her feet felt so heavy, almost impossible to lift.

Sure, Drew and she were no longer living in the same building anymore, but they both had phones. She could have called Drew today, asked him to join her. But too used to hollering down from the third floor to the second, "Put it in motion, Chandler, we're ripping up the asphalt in five minutes" she hadn't picked up the phone, hadn't made the extra effort that change always required.

Then again, he could have picked up the phone, too, and called her to make arrangements.

He hadn't.

Drew never did anything extra, placing a phone call falling under that general heading.

And she...well, she followed certain rules of conduct.

The end result was—set in old patterns of behavior, neither of them had done anything.

So now she ran alone.

Without Drew there to egg her on, to make her laugh, to insist she continue, sadness caught up with her.

Damn him! He should have called. It was his place to call, his place to make the first move. He was the one who had packed up and moved out. *He* had left *her*. For a man who shunned both socks and underwear, who was a self-admitted slug, he had certainly jumped when it came to finding a new address. He couldn't get away from her fast enough. It was almost as though he'd been waiting for the opportunity to ditch her.

Had he been looking for an out? Deep down, was he relieved to rid himself of the ol' ball and chain? Is that why he had agreed to show her the sexual ropes, so he could palm her off on another guy and walk away, guilt free?

Oh God. What if she never saw Drew again? How would she ever bear it?

A burning sensation started behind her eyeballs.

The breeze off the pond, she decided. It was a windy day, a good day for sailing. That's why so many colorful sails dotted the water. That's why her eyes were filling up. Gusts of wind blew dust into her eyes.

Beside a grove of cedars, her breathing turned labored. She couldn't go on, couldn't continue, couldn't act as though nothing was wrong when everything was wrong, when her whole world was falling apart.

Sadness overtaking her, tears gaining, almost winning, Kesley stopped running. No slow down first. Staggering into the cool green shade, she stumbled against a cedar and pressed her forehead to the tree's rough bark.

Don't cry…don't cry…*you mustn't cry, Kesley*…

From behind her, a hand palmed her shoulder, rubbed her back. "I saw you coming around the bend like a bat outta hell. What I tell you about running too fast?"

Drew! Speaking low, his soothing voice calming her.

"Don't force it," he ordered. "Don't try and make it happen. Just let the air into your lungs naturally."

"I—I…"

"No talking. Just catch your breath."

She nodded.

"I dropped by the apartment," he said, still rubbing her back as she tried to drag oxygen into her lungs. "But you had already left. Why didn't you wait? You should've waited for me, Kes. I'm your partner. Talking with a partner helps a runner keep to an easy pace."

Fearing he'd be a no-show, she'd left. Better to leave, she reasoned, than wait and chance disappointment.

Oh, God! She should have trusted him not to leave her hanging. She should have known he'd be there for her. When had Drew ever left her in the lurch?

Her micro-poly fabric top, designed to wick moisture away from the skin, worked well against the normal perspiration of running, but failed miserably against clammy, fear-driven sweat. When Drew lifted her top up and away from her back, the pond's cool breeze felt wonderful against her spine, as did the warmer puffs of Drew's exhales. Both dried the stress-induced droplets clinging to her skin, but only one made her wet.

She remembered Drew's breaths on her flesh during sex, recalled his whispers of encouragement that first time. He was doing it again, blowing puffs of air across her feverish skin, encouraging her. And just like before, her excitement soared.

"Undo my bra," she said, giving into her reckless urge.

Sex would keep the sadness away.

Drew's fingers hovered uncertainly at the clasp of her bra, before freeing her from the restriction of white nylon.

The sun melted to a sliver of gold toffee on the horizon and darkness moved in, but their surroundings no longer mattered. Their whereabouts had faded from her consciousness. Only the fresh smell of cedar and the touch of his hand circling her back, skin against skin, permeated her senses.

"That's good. That's good, sweetheart," he whispered. "Just let everything go. Whatever is riding you, just put it away, until you can breathe."

The very real possibility of losing him was riding her. The thought of never seeing him again had sent her into a panic. She couldn't let the grief go, couldn't let *him* go, even though in her heart of hearts she knew releasing both was the right thing to do. Understanding intellectually that this change in their lives was all for the best, because Drew didn't want what she wanted, that they didn't share the same vision of the future, did little to assuage her misery.

All they had was now. Right this very moment. Soon, they might both go off in opposite directions.

"Help me take off my top." She raised both hands over her head to make its removal easier.

"Here? You want your top off here?"

She gave a desperate, "Yes"

"Kes, there's no privacy here."

"No one ever leaves the trails. Except lovers. Are we lovers, Drew?"

"What a short memory you have, my sweet. Either that, or the occasion wasn't nearly as memorable for you as for me."

Drew was trying to jolly her out of her blue mood doldrums. The occasion couldn't have been *memorable* for him, as he had great sex all the time. Though she appreciated his trying to cheer her up, trying to make her feel better, his well-meaning attempt wouldn't work, not this time. Only sex would make her feel good.

She put him on the spot. "Are we in sex mode now?"

"Do you want us to be in sex mode now, Kesley?"

Drew had used her full name. This meant he was abandoning humor and taking her seriously. "Yes, I want us in sex mode. And Drew—I need hard. No more virgin sex for me."

He plucked at the hem of her top, debating the wisdom of its removal most likely. Why debate? There was absolutely nothing wise about any of this, and she didn't care. She only cared about having sex with Drew. Someday, when she was a lonely old woman, she would look back upon her life and recall their wild time together in the green cedars. The happy memory would chase the sadness away.

"My place isn't far," he argued. "We can get there in under a minute."

"No. Here," she insisted. "I don't care if anybody sees." Time to break old, safe patterns of behavior. "Please?" she sobbed out.

"Don't cry, Kes." A pleading note had crept into his voice. "I'll do whatever you want, you know that."

"Then do this."

With a protracted sigh of resignation, he removed her top.

A roll of her shoulders sent the bra to the ground. Naked from the waist up, she stretched out her arms against the tree, her breasts swinging free. "I need a man, Drew."

When he didn't touch her or say anything, she deliberately let her engorged nipples scrape the rough cedar bark. The pain felt good. One hurt substituted for another hurt, helping her forget the other, more severe pain of a future without Drew.

"Don't do that," he cried. "You'll hurt yourself."

Pulling her away from the rough bark, Drew reached around her torso and flicked his large thumbs across her breasts. The nipples lengthened an enormous degree.

"Harder" Her forehead fell forward against the tree. "Do me harder."

When he pinched and pulled the areola she felt only relief. "Do dirty things to me, Drew. Make me do dirty things to you. Force me. I want raunchy sex."

"Kesley, listen…"

"Please," she begged.

She heard the quickening of his breath, felt a hand push low over her belly and tunnel under the elastic waist of her black jogging shorts.

"I told you no bra," he said, his voice changing from concerned to curt. "And you wore a bra."

"I'm sorry. I didn't know I'd be seeing you this evening."

"Here on out, you are to be prepared for me. Always. Day or night. Or you will raise my ire."

Ire? When had that word ever been a part of Drew's vocabulary?

But… "All right" she quickly agreed, while intending to raise more than Drew's *ire*.

Large fingers splayed her bottom, between poly-fiber and cotton. "Panties too." Drew tssked in a very unlike Drew way. "I told you, no underwear. You disobeyed me."

"I'm sorry, so sorry," she whispered. A shiver of excitement raced through her, faster than her feet had run around Jamaica Pond, anticipation of sex outdistancing the encroaching sadness. In the here and now, she was Drew's woman. And she felt that ownership as he reached around to her front and ungently ground his palm into her mons.

"From now on, you'll keep your cunt bare."

"Yes, Drew. I promise, Drew."

"Not good enough. You require disciplining." He dragged her jogging shorts down her legs. "I need to punish you."

"For crissakes, the panties are white too," he said in disgust. "Nice girl's white panties. Not even black lace, French cut. Not even a thong."

"I'm sorry," she said again as he peeled the plain white panties down over her rump.

The breeze off the pond feathered across her bottom cheeks as he bared her buttocks outside in the grove of cedar trees, where a jogger running the nearby track or anyone walking through the woods might see.

At the level of her upper thighs, the descent of both her shorts and panties stopped, and his hand came down on her bared bottom. Hard. Again and again.

Her knuckles muffled her screams. Tears streaming down her face, dropping off her chin, she felt the horrible knot of tension release inside her.

Afterwards, while she cried softly, he kissed her flaming bottom, his mouth appeasing the ache, his tongue flicking across her bruised flesh, the relief like an ice cube applied to the heat of a sunburn.

"Oh, God," she moaned, and clawed the cedar's bark, her sensual gratification intense. In a life riddled with convention, she needed this.

Forgetting the future, abandoning herself to the now, Kesley gave her body over to him, ten years worth of trust culminating in unreserved capitulation.

Drew would never hurt her. She could act freely with him, surrender to him, show him her true self. He'd keep her safe, never betray her weakness or even see her need as weakness. The most accepting person she had ever known, the least judgmental, Drew conducted his life only in the present. He of all people would understand her need to stay in the moment.

When his teeth scraped her, her own teeth clenched in an agony of rapture. "Yes, yes, yes," she quaked. "Do me like that, hard like that. Bite me."

He did. Oh, he did. He gave her everything she needed, and more. And she wondered, stripped down and defenseless, as he held her sanity in his hand, if he would go as far with her as she would go with him.

"It's okay to want to escape everything and everyone else, sweetheart, but don't try escaping me. I won't be shut out of your fantasy. I'll do whatever you want as long as you know it's me."

"I'd never do that." As he stood up, she turned to face him, locked into him, blind to everything else but him. "It's you! *You* are my fantasy"

"Then tell me what you want me to do."

Even with his usual elegant slouch, Drew towered over her. There was no mistaking his strength, not when muscles bulged beneath his sleeveless tee shirt. Her shorts now lassoed her upper thighs, and his gaze sank to her bared pussy. Physically weak, emotionally spent, and almost naked, she felt perfectly safe.

"Please, Drew, let me…" She couldn't complete the request. Couldn't put the desire into words. Her own strength had always been effective communication, and here she was suddenly tongue-tied.

Taking charge of the situation, he unzipped in one smooth motion. "Take it out."

Too awed for subtlety, she did. Clumsily.

Drew was a spectacular sight, his penis erect and thick, pointing at her, the length impressive. Unsure of how to proceed, she touched him with an eager finger. Had she done it wrong? She felt so gauche. Knowing what she *wanted* to do and enacting the fantasy were two different things.

"Cup my balls," he ordered. At her timid squeeze, he added, "I'll stop you long before you break anything."

She gladly followed the instruction. In fact, biting her lip, she went a little berserk.

He groaned. "Fuck, what you do to me."

False praise. She wasn't doing anything except getting to know his lovely thick cock, the acquaintance done with various hand motions, some fast, some slow, some delicate, some a little rough. Curious about the liquid beading the tip—yes, she knew it was pre-cum, but how did it taste?—Kesley dipped at the waist to find out.

"Before you suck me off, get naked."

"Pardon?" She blinked.

"You heard me. Everything off. Stripped to the skin. That's the only way you'll get it."

Still palming his testicles, admiring their weighty presence in her hand— he was unexpectedly heavy—she shimmied out of the shorts. Wearing only sneakers and socks, she sank to her knees. In that position, she looked up to him for further coaching.

His hooded eyes seared her to the core. "Open your legs."

She parted her knees.

"You're wet," he said.

"You bring out the submissive in me," she breathlessly conceded.

"You, a submissive? Ha! In my dreams, you're a submissive. During my awake time, I know you like calling the shots. Even kneeling on the ground, you're the one on top here."

She admitted to difficulties around control issues, she did tend to micro-manage all the details of her overly cluttered, overly scheduled life. But this exercise wasn't about holding on. This exercise was about letting go. And not of control.

Of Drew.

Chapter Twenty

Drew put himself away. Well, well, *hell*, well.

Though not the most technically expert blowjob he'd ever received, Kesley's BJ scored right up there with the most enthusiastic. And who needed by-the-numbers anyway, when the top of his head was exploding?

His little sweetheart had a real feel for the erotic. Her untutored excitement, the way her pink tongue slid down his cock—the deal was nearly all over for him before she took him into her mouth.

He never would have asked her to perform oral sex on him, particularly not in the great outdoors where they ran the risk of arrest. But unwilling to put a damper on her enthusiasm with petty details like getting his butt thrown in jail, he let her use him as fantasy fodder. After she'd put up with his ass dragging for ten years, he figured satisfying her carnal imaginings was the least he could do. For sure, Kes had some stuff to work through before realizing she loved him, so he'd go along—

Up to a point.

That point being letting her go. He wasn't letting Kes go. Not to another man, not for any reason. Kes was all his.

That said, he hoped and prayed he would never let her down. He'd turn himself inside out so as not to disappoint Kes. If it took his dying breath, he'd live up to this woman's expectations. If not for her, if not for trying to be a better man for her, he would have amounted to a big fat zero.

Lurking beneath her enjoyment of the sex, she was plenty steamed with him. Perhaps pissed with his silence on the "L" word. He couldn't say he blamed her. There were reasons for his indecision, for his slowness in committing to her, reasons for his reluctance to go to the next level. And sometimes it took a knock over the head to bring a man to his senses.

Ted was his knock. Truthfully, the knock was more like a sledgehammer to the skull. Ted woke Drew up to the reality that if he didn't act, he'd lose his miracle.

That would be Kes.

He didn't deserve her—that was a no brainer. But years ago, he'd stopped beating himself up any time luck just happened to go his way. No longer questioning fate, he now humbly accepted his good fortune with gratitude…and no boat rocking.

If it ain't broke don't fix it—that was his motto. And what they'd had was perfect. Why screw with perfect?

So in ten years of perfect togetherness, they hadn't had sex. Big fucking deal. Couples regularly having great sex split up all the time. As far as he could tell, sex, or the lack thereof, meant little to the success of a relationship. If a decade together didn't constitute a commitment what the hell did?

Kes had been right about the moving angle. But moving had meant making a decision about the future, about them. Moving had meant screwing with perfect, and doing that took a lot of faith and hope and trust. He wasn't too big on intangibles.

But he was real big on Kes.

She was his tangible, his proof that in a rotten world miracles existed.

The sight of her. The lush sight of her Her mouth. His cock delving between her lips, her lips kissing him. Her tongue. Licking him, tasting him, circling the hard perimeter of him before lapping him from base to head. Sex with Kes was more than a miracle. Sex with Kes was heaven on earth.

He told her he'd stop her before she broke his balls, and that was his only for-real instruction, given so a limp dick wouldn't spoil her fun. He had never gone too deep into the S and M scene. Pain was not his thing.

Evidently, it was hers.

At first, he thought he might have been mistaken—this was his saintly Kes, after all. But after gauging her responsiveness, he quickly determined that yeah, she had a thing for spankings. As he lived to pleasure Kes, he would naturally comply with her desires.

He had to admit that, at least today, smacking her ass had held some appeal. When she went off trail, running at a breakneck speed, he thought for sure something bad had happened to her. With his heart dropped to his toes, he would have gladly taken her over his knee then. But spanking was as far as he was venturing into S and M. For them, he wanted a white picket fence and a happily ever after, not leather and whips.

Drew helped his sweetheart to her feet and got her dressed. Then kissed her cheek. "Thank you."

Licking her lips, she grinned. "You're welcome."

Yes indeedy, Kes was very pleased with herself. Why had he ever feared ruining things with sex? Things had never looked better.

During the short drive back to his house, closer than her apartment, she turned remote, not a good sign in a talkative lady like his sweetheart. Her silence prompted him to ask, "How's work going with you? Any problems with the kids?"

"Fine. Everything is fine."

He didn't think so.

Right there and then, Drew decided to move up his last business trip. That way, he would be around when she needed him. He'd lay odds that kid in her caseload was about to run.

"Kes, I'm leaving Sunday morning for a consulting job. I'm sorry. I know it's earlier than I told you, but the trip can't be helped." He'd work around the clock to finish up ahead of schedule so that things could get resolved between them. No sense delaying any longer. He wanted this beautiful, pigheaded woman married to him so he could shower her with everything she deserved. For the sake of his sanity, he needed things squared away soon.

Her bottom lip trembled. "In that case, I think I will spend the night. We'll end it between us Sunday morning. Closure."

Closure. He fucking hated that word. That word did not apply to them. They weren't ending. They were only just beginning.

With a yank on the steering wheel, Drew pulled into the driveway and cut the engine.

She cocked a too-bright eye at him. "Since this is our last time together, how about we get adventurous?"

"What did you have in mind?"

"Bondage."

He let out a sigh. "I don't do bondage."

"I hear people talk. Everybody does bondage. It's the flavor of the month."

"Nope. Not me. I like vanilla. I prefer just you and me coming together," he said, offering her no other inducement except his love.

"But you must have sex toys in the house, right?"

"No accoutrements."

"This is not what I heard about you. I heard toys."

"And I told you, people exaggerate."

"The thing you do with the feather. We can try that."

She wasn't listening He was coming clean and she refused to hear. "It was a quill from an antique fountain pen."

"Wow! I'm game."

"Kes, look at me. Really look at me. Do I look like the type of guy who would own an antique fountain pen? I'm a ballpoint pen type of guy."

"Okay, so we'll improvise. And don't tell me you don't have any feathers in the house because I know you prefer feather pillows to synthetics. We can grab a handful from there."

A handful?

He cringed. Many lonely nights spent in a motel room had gone into the making of that little ditty about the quill. In the context of that piece of fiction, one feather was a stretch. A handful would kill any mortal man. Why had his so-called friends picked that tall-tale to tell Kes? Why not relate the anecdote with the cucumber dildo? In theory at least, that fabrication was doable. Besides which, he had just stocked his fridge with salad fixings. "Kes, about the feather pillows—I threw them out."

"What!"

"I bought hyper-allergenic pillows for the bed." Feathers made Kes sneeze. "Besides, they were the wrong kind of feathers. Guess we'll just have to go retro with old-fashioned lovemaking."

Kes made her mad face at him, and then, without waiting for him to come around and open the door, slammed out of the van and stormed for the house.

Not exactly how he'd pictured the first night of their new life together.

◆ ◆ ◆

So that was that, Kesley thought, racing up the drive. One more night together, and they would go their separate ways. They hadn't even lasted the specified two weeks. Ten years together platonically, not even fourteen days together as lovers. Disappointment didn't come close to describing her frame of mind.

And that was her issue, her problem entirely.

But she couldn't help thinking that if the world had been a different place, the outcome between them would have been different too. She had to face reality—the number of commitment phobes had reached epidemic proportions. People fell in love all the time, but few stayed in love forever. Or even 'til Monday morning.

Weekend relationships. How could dating be any other way, when saying "I do" at the altar was no guarantee of anything?

"Come back here, Kesley."

Sucking up the tears, she turned. "What do you want?"

"I want you to have faith in me. Do you have faith in me, Kesley?"

Drew stood beside his brand-new car, in his brand-new driveway, at his brand new address, in this swanky brand-new part of town, and he wanted her to have faith in him? "What kind of a question is that?"

"Well, do you have faith in me? Or after ten years, are you finally punking out on me?"

She took a quivery breath. Drew had always been her bulwark on shifting sands. Through thick and thin, sick or healthy, he had been her constant, the one person she knew she could always depend upon to be there for her. She had believed in him since the moment they met. "I have always had faith in you."

Two forceful strides brought the man who never hurried to her side. He pushed her too-long bangs aside. "Then tell me what's bothering you."

Her bottom lip trembled. "No."

"Then let it all go. Just for the night, give yourself over to me. Completely. I not only want your faith, I want everything you've got to give. In fact, I demand it. Put everything else aside, and concentrate on letting me make you feel good. Put your faith in that. I can make you feel so nice, sweetheart," he promised, kissing her earlobe.

When Drew took her lips in a deep drugging kiss, Kesley melted. "Mmm. Oh, yes. Mmm. Yes."

High on Drew, her opiate of choice, she lost all awareness. Had they walked side by side to the house? Had he carried her? Had they danced up the driveway?

Somehow—she didn't know how—they ended up inside the kitchen. Amidst the shadowy shapes of unpacked moving boxes, proof that Drew had moved on, started a new life without her, she attacked him. Ripping at buttons and zippers and shoelaces, she couldn't wait to get at all that warm male skin underneath. He mirrored her actions, until they were both naked.

Purposely, she let the peaks of her breasts skim the wall of his chest, trembling at the resultant ache that started at the tips and culminated in her vagina. He trembled too as she shimmied her body up and down his body, nuzzling his smooth chest, her lips covering one flat nipple, suckling him, nipping him, tonguing him.

Hard. *Harder!*

Anger and fear, and loss rose up within her. Ugly emotions she never even knew she possessed. Venting on his flesh, she clawed him. Bit him. A sad frenzy, a horrible frustration, an unleashed fury that nothing would abate—

Except sex.

"Fuck me, Drew. No romance. No let up 'til morning. Can you do that for me?"

"No problem."

Evidently, Drew hadn't had time to relocate three "shorty" wardrobe boxes from the kitchen to the appropriate closets. The squat cubes waited together in the middle of the floor, like a train in a station. When he lifted her up onto the first one, she wanted to cry, "All aboard".

And then she just wanted to cry. Period.

The boxes seemed like an omen of things to come. For what was less permanent than cardboard, more temporary than packing material, more transient than a train waiting in a station? After sorting through the contents, he would throw the boxes away. Dispose of the packing material without another thought.

Would he do the same with her?

The corrugation of the cardboard felt rough under her bare bottom. She liked it. When Drew separated her legs with a knee, the action also rough, she liked that too.

He stepped between her legs. Her feet dangling over the edge of the box, he pushed two ungentle fingers up inside her. "You're dripping."

"Yes."

"Lean back on your elbows," he ordered.

Thankfully, the three joined boxes made for a large, even spacious, bed. With plenty of room to spare on the top flaps, she collapsed backward onto the boxes and bent her arms. Boneless with inertia, she arched her throat, and her mouth gaped, her legs splayed for him. The sloppy, squishy, sucking sounds of vaginal wetness soon filled the dark kitchen as he pushed her to the edge of climax.

Drew knew exactly what he was doing, which buttons to push and how to push them. Only when she begged him for release, pleading "Please, please, please" did he snap her over the precipice. The tears started then. She sobbed as she came.

And he continued to move his two fingers within her body's clasp.

"Come inside me," she cried raggedly. "Please come inside me."

"Pull your feet up on top of the box," her cruel dictator said. "Heels at the edge."

How lewd, she thought, and rushed to comply.

"Am I open enough?" she anxiously asked, arranging her body for his taking, wishing only to please him, as he had just pleased her. Would he *please, please, please*, hurry up and please her again?

Relief arrived when the blunt head of his penis circled her opening. "Once you start, Drew, don't stop. Fuck me all night long."

Chapter Twenty-One

Kesley didn't know the hour, didn't really care to know. In the dark bedroom, lost to everything but Drew, time had stopped.

"Where are you going?" she asked lazily when the mattress shifted, signifying Drew was leaving the bed.

"To light a few candles."

By the glow of a dozen flickering flames, she watched the tall, blond, strikingly handsome man make his way back to her.

Drew looked huge. And hugely erect. How handsome he was, how gracefully he moved. The man was perfect in every way, while she was a mess. Sweaty and lust-scented. Plain, even on a good day, and this was the worst day of her life. Drew was leaving her.

To mask the sadness, she smiled gaily as he took her in his arms.

"Christ, Kes," he rasped, entering her body once again, hard, and thrusting deep, driving, pushing, pounding her to the edge of climax. "What you do to me."

Afterwards, she slept. When she awakened, Kesley sensed she was alone in the master bedroom.

She stretched out an arm, only to make sure her lover hadn't retreated all the way to the far side of the mattress, only to confirm her initial instinct: She slept alone in the huge antique bed.

After the last time, Drew was still tellingly erect. He'd wanted more sex, but she'd let sleep claim her. That wouldn't happen again.

She padded naked through the dark hallways, a mellow glow drawing her to the library. Sprawled on a red velvet cushioned window seat, wearing faded black jeans and an unbuttoned white shirt, Drew read by the light of a single candle.

At her knock, he looked up at her. A very masculine strip of leather held his place in the story as he placed his book aside.

She stayed by the door, raised a hand to her messy hair, tucking a lank strand behind an ear. "Sorry for interrupting."

His eyes, at half-mast and full of desire, settled *eventually* on her face. "You could never interrupt. I was only reading to pass the time while you slept."

"About that…I knew you wanted to—you know—but the warmth of your body, the comfort of your beating heart, lulled me to sleep. After telling you not to quit, I reneged on my end of the bargain. I apologize."

"Never apologize to me again, Kes. Especially not about sex. I'm glad you got some rest in my arms, in my bed."

She took a bold step closer to the window seat. "I'm awake now."

"So you are." He held out a hand to her. When their fingers linked, he pulled her towards him.

Drew was highly charged sexually, with conquests all over the country. She didn't want to disappoint him. She didn't want to disappoint herself. How to tell him she trusted him not to hurt her, no matter how outrageous things got between them? This was her last chance to be with Drew, and she had a horrible compulsion to try everything, to do it all, no restrictions. Would he allow everything? Would he answer her most hidden and secret needs?

Only one way to find out—

She climbed up onto the loveseat with him, a knee on either side of his hips, bracketing him. Her breasts shifting, swaying, the hard nipples stroking his chest, she brushed her lips to his mouth. "Right here on the window seat."

"You got it," he said, and unzipped.

But for all the agreement of those words, for all the speed with which he'd released his remarkable erection from the enclosure of his jeans, those words had not been said with ease. His vocal cords sounded hoarse. Lack of sleep?

Or lack of desire?

Sure, his penis jutted, but his male physiology, his sexual stamina, proved nothing. She didn't take his arousal personally. Drew didn't really want *her*. Drew just wanted a woman. Any woman would do.

She held herself steady, as his hands smoothed over her, sculpting her too small breasts, kneading her belly, stroking her pussy, until she shuddered and quaked and writhed above him.

"I'm dying without you. Take me, woman, and be quick about it."

To make it easy for him to pretend he was with someone else, a sultry siren, the type of female she wasn't and would never be—Drew's type of woman—she said, "Blow out the candle first."

◆ ◆ ◆

When the real estate agent had shown Drew the house, the library had closed the deal. He liked to read, and at the time, he'd pictured tons of books lining the shelves.

Kes had changed all that. Now, he knew he'd never picture this room again without seeing his sweetheart in it.

His shy woman had asked him to blow out the candle. He hadn't wanted to, but knowing Kes was new to sex, he'd complied. Lucky for him, he had great night vision. Otherwise, he would have missed her rapt expression as she rode him, clothed in nothing but streaming moonlight.

But first, before riding him, she'd tortured him.

His hot eyes had turned to slits, his chest had heaved like a sick bull, as she'd masturbated him. "Keep doing what you're doing, sweetheart," he'd croaked, letting her hear him sounding weak and hungry, letting her take charge. "Yeah, oh yeah," he'd groaned.

Cradling his balls, milking his cock good and hard, she did whatever she wanted to do to him—

While his own hands hung at his sides.

As helpless as a babe, as turned-on as only a man can be, so owned by her that he might just as well have hung a "Sold" sign around his neck, he let her take him.

Fierce. His woman was fierce. No question about it, she slayed him. Death by sex—he had no complaints.

For himself.

But things had started getting a little wild, and he was apprehensive for her sake.

Later, while touring the room by candlelight, looking at books, reading off titles, the urge had struck. A kiss, then full progression from there. With a sigh, Kes backed up against the front of his jeans.

"Kes," he whispered in her ear, running both hands over her arms, "we keep this up, and you won't be able to walk come morning."

"I don't care."

He molded her backside, cupped her ass cheek. Dipping his knees, he kissed his way down her spine, mouthed his way back up again. Lifting the hair off her nape, he bit her, like a stud bites a mare during the mating approach. He'd never understood before, but he understood now, why stallions made those nips.

The room steamed with lust. Her skin dripped with the dew of her perspiration. He was doing his fair share of sweating too. They'd been going at it all night. No let-up, since Kes came to him in the library. Drew had a sinking feeling this wouldn't be the last time either. Nothing could've prevented him from having Kes again.

Except the lady herself.

"You sure?" he asked. Snaking a hand around to her front, he squeezed a dainty tit.

Her breasts drove him wild, especially the nipples. Hard and long, astounding in size. A woman as tiny as Kes had no business having such big nipples.

She let her head fall back against his shoulder. "Mmm, I'm sure."

Leaving go of her nipple, he pushed the heel of his hand down her front, belly to pussy.

Kes was wet, her cunt honey-slick.

His greedy cock leapt for joy. "Let's go back to bed, sweetheart."

"No. Right here. Right now."

Vertical wasn't easy. But Kes was small, and he could easily lift her. With her legs wrapped around him, they'd make do, especially with her back against a wall for support—

"I want it all, Drew. First, from the rear. Then, anal."

He gulped. *Oh*—

Kes was turning out to be one adventurous wench.

He eyed her graceful back, her beautiful ass, her shapely thighs parted in welcome. Was the room hotter than before or was he on fire?

♦ ♦ ♦

In the library, Drew took her from the rear while she stood facing the wall. Slightly bent at the waist, he had come into her with gentle deliberation, his strokes carefully measured.

At least, at first.

Then, nice-guy Drew snapped. Pulling her away from the wall, he'd rounded her over so that her fingers touched her toes—the dirty position just what she needed.

Drew was not quite as pleased. Actually, he seemed furious with her.

They'd gone at it like animals—wild animals, not the tame version kept behind bars at a zoo—not once but twice, and in quick-fire succession. Afterwards, to cool off, they'd gone swimming naked outdoors in the in-ground pool, skinny-dipping in the dark, once again, just the kind of naughtiness she had craved. Refreshed and invigorated, they ran hand-in-hand for the house.

Drew insisted they return to the bedroom.

"I want anal with you," he said, sounding bemused. "I usually don't."

"Oh, no?" she said, curious about his revelation and curious, too, how they could so openly discuss anal intercourse and yet could not discuss his past or their lack of a future. "Why not? Too labor intensive, Mr. Slip-On Loafers?"

He chuckled. "Something like that."

As she kneed the bed, getting up on all fours, she heard him swallow from his standing position behind her.

"Bring your hips up," he said.

"Like this?" She raised her bottom.

"More. So I can see it go in."

The visual thing again.

Smiling, she hiked her bottom high.

She enjoyed sex, at least she did with Drew, and she purred her appreciation into the pillow, her bottom raised, her lover's heavy breathing praise in and of itself. Sensual, powerful, confident of her own sexuality, at that moment, she felt more than pretty…

For the first time in her life, she felt beautiful.

"Oh, yes," she said and licked her lips, loving the tension building inside her but not nearly as much as she loved the man providing that tension. When he ministered to her with fragrant oils, slipping in a finger, ecstasy loomed on the horizon, and she rolled her hips in earthy delight.

Something wider, thicker, replaced the digit. Something that insistently prodded her buttocks.

His cock.

"You feel so good, so good," he moaned, and made the penetration.

She shuddered as her body drew him in, shuddered and quaked, and loved it, sobbing just how much she loved it, her ass filled with him, his hands all over her, his mouth open on her nape, his teeth bared against her skin, their bodies moving in perfect rhythm right up to the moment they both screamed.

♦ ♦ ♦

Kes turned to him. "I should go. You need to get to the airport."

Drew forgot how to breathe. He tugged her closer, not wanting her to go anywhere. Not ever.

"It's only just dawn." He kissed her jaw. "We still have a couple of hours. There's time."

She jumped off the bed and into her clothes. "You might have time, but I have a ton of things to do. My singles meeting is tonight and I can't do a thing with my hair. My salon appointment is way overdue."

What?

She sounded like she was cutting him out of her life the same way she was cutting her hair. They'd just spent the night together. Didn't making love mean the same to her as to him?

Evidently not.

"Thanks Drew. For everything. Don't bother seeing me to the door."

He couldn't believe his ears. She was dismissing them—dismissing *him*—like he was nothing but garbage, worthless trash that got chucked like a used condom. Is that all he was to her? A cock with no man attached?

When the door closed behind Kes, it all came down on him. Everything bad that had ever been done to him as a little boy, all the rotten stuff he'd had to do on the streets as a kid to get by, all the shitty crap he'd been through as a young man, the degradation he tried not to think about—all of it hit him at once.

As Kes breezed out of his life, Drew crumbled facedown on the bed he had bought for them to share.

-195-

Chapter Twenty-Two

Kesley flipped back the bedcovers and dragged her leaden body upright. Next step was throwing her weighted legs over the side of the mattress.

Ugh! Everything she owned hurt. Maybe she had the flu—

She tottered to the window and pulled up the shade.

Big mistake, second only to glancing outside.

A dark depressing sky met her gritty eyes. As far as she could see, gray clouds hung low over the city.

Looked like rain. Better pack the umbrella.

Hell, the rain and overcast skies would most likely last all day. Maybe all week. Good weather was gone in the wink of an eye, but nasty weather tended to hang on forever…

Griping to herself, she headed for the bathroom. Her walk mimicked the gait of the walking wounded.

"Sometimes life just plain sucks," she whined aloud as she soaped up under the shower spray.

Going through the motions, she wrapped her wet hair in a towel, used another to dry off. Everything required effort. Everything tired her out, even breathing. She should just return to bed and yank the damn bedcovers over her wet head.

And that would be just so incredibly weak and self-indulgent.

So—just like the day before, and the day before that, she would force herself to go to work, pretend to be a part of it all, when she wasn't feeling like a part of anything. One week after Drew's departure from her life, she felt nothing. Absolutely nothing. Except numb. Dead inside. Like she was on the outside of life looking in. Was she even visible?

Her morning shower had fogged up the bathroom mirror. To reassure herself she still existed, Kesley wiped the steam from the glass and hunted down her reflection.

And there she was, all right, staring back from the mirror. A hollowed-cheeked, shadowed-eyed, thirty-year old wreck of a woman—she had duly noted her painful existence on the planet.

Unwrapping the terrycloth turban, Kesley performed the same-old-same-old routine, blotting the lank strands with the towel, combing out the knots, kicking herself for not making an appointment at the salon for that much-needed trim, the haircut she'd been putting off for weeks, the one she had told Drew about that last day they were together.

Drew—

Her knees sagged, her shoulders slumped. Standing upright required a real balancing act.

No! She couldn't think of Drew.

Drew was her drug of choice, her addiction. To get clean and sober, she had to go cold turkey. No thoughts of Drew, not one.

Kesley determinedly raked a comb through the snarls, the tug on her scalp causing her sleep-deprived eyes to smart.

She wished she could cry. Wished she could let it all out. Wished the tears would fall, while knowing not even a good, long, self-pitying crying jag would help.

Some wounds never healed. Not even with the passage of time. Because some wounds weren't a clean cut. Some wounds punctured a person in such a way that no amount of bandages or stitches or marked off boxes on a calendar could hold the jagged edges together.

And some wounds, like losing Drew in her life, were too deep for the healing balm of tears.

All she could do was put one foot down before the other, and get through each endless, cloudy day.

Letting Drew go had been the right thing to do. She had no claims on him. They'd had sex a few times. So what? They'd made a deal, and the deal had stuck.

Why hadn't she known that sex would change things between them?

Drew had warned her, and she'd refused to listen. He'd been trying to tell her something, and she wouldn't hear. Not until it was too late to save her heart, had she finally understood he'd been trying to tell her was goodbye.

So, to save them both a messy scene, she'd said goodbye first.

And now, she had to finish getting ready for work. A full morning of appointments and group meetings lay ahead of her. In the afternoon, John was scheduled to come into The Shelter to sign up for a program.

That piece of optimism kept her going.

Chapter Twenty-Three

Cosmopolitan storefronts dotted both sides of Centre Street, the main retail district in Jamaica Plain. The grocery shops—some expensive and gourmet, some cheap and funky—represented every ethnic taste. The same eclectic diversity held true for the bars and cafes and restaurants.

Once, Drew had tried to count the different languages he heard on the sidewalk or saw in print at the corner newsstand, only to decide every dialect under the sun could be had on the busy street. Barbershops and beauty parlors made a bundle catering to the wants of their hodgepodge clientele, straightening kinky hair, kinking up straight hair, dying and cutting every length and texture of hair.

A mixed bag of skin pigments and incomes and social strata and sexual orientation and age groups walked this one, long, *alive* street. From well-heeled, briefcase carrying lawyers to the downtrodden homeless shuffling along with a bagful of earthly possessions, from textbook toting college students to old folks pushing two-wheeled metal shopping carts. Jamaica Plain lived and breathed and celebrated its multi-cultural citizenry, joyfully thumbing its collective noses at suburban homogeneity.

While waiting outside the world's best ice cream parlor, Drew acknowledged he couldn't live anywhere else.

Unless he lived there with Kes.

He'd live anywhere then. Who cared where the welcome mat sat as long as the door he walked through brought him to her?

Drew checked his watch.

Kes must be running late. 'Course, he'd arrived extra early. Here's hoping she'd got his message about meeting him here…

He'd hauled ass from Logan sometime after midnight, too late for a visit, but not for touching base through the phone lines or microwaves. Just as he'd done several times a day for the past week, he'd picked up the phone and had himself a nice one-way chat with Kesley's answering machine.

She hadn't returned any of his calls. Would she meet him today or blow him off again?

He was edging towards discouragement when he caught a glimpse of a real beauty walking towards him down the sidewalk. Wearing a stylish purple silk scarf wound Parisian-style around her lovely throat, a skinny straight black skirt and tall high heels, she looked as sophisticated as the street they both loved.

Kes!

Regardless of how beautiful she looked, even at a distance, Drew could tell things weren't going too swell with his sweetheart.

Worried for her, happy to see her, and so much in love with her…he raced to meet her.

Rather than the warm kiss on the lips they usually exchanged, she dodged his mouth and raised her cheek.

"I missed you," he blurted despite the lip rejection. "You look different."

"I lightened my hair and did some shopping on Newbury Street." She smiled an Acting Class 101 sort of smile and spun in place. "You like?"

"I always like how you look. You're a knockout, Kesley."

"Thank you. That's so sweet. Ted likes the new me too. I did the makeover for him a few days ago. He likes blondes."

Ted. The bogus shit. The hemorrhoid asshole. What did Drew care what that little fuck liked? And Kes shouldn't care either.

Suddenly, the boxy lump in Drew's pocket matched the lump in his throat. Had Kes and Ted become lovers while he'd been gone?

To hide his worry, anger and jealousy too, Drew looked down, trying hard to blot out the image of Kesley with the smarmy jerk, Ted.

"How's about an ice cream?" he asked the sidewalk. "Double scoop chocolate mocha cone, my treat. I'll try not to get any jimmies stuck to my chin like I usually do."

"No, I'm afraid I can't. Ted and I have a date tonight and I need to clear out my desk at work before he comes over to the apartment."

"Clear out your desk? What the hell are you talking about, clear out your desk? Where are you going?" He nodded. "Oh, I get it. You're finally getting a larger office, right?"

"Actually, no. I'm taking a leave of absence. The job just drains me, you know? And I decided it was time for a break."

"What the frig? I know you've been feeling stressed lately, but that will pass with time. And you love your work. You're damned good at it too. But I can understand your needing to take a vacation—everyone needs to recharge their batteries and you don't take nearly enough time away from the job—but to outright quit and walk away." He shook his head back and forth, trying to understand what had come over her, and failing. "It just doesn't sound like you to make a rash decision like this."

"It's not rash. The decision only seems hasty on the outside. The truth is, I've been reassessing my career path for a long time."

Stunned, he said, "I didn't know. What are you thinking about doing instead?"

"I'm thinking law school come fall. Ease into it gradually, take a few night courses, work part-time someplace during the day."

"You want to be a lawyer?" He felt his face contort. "But Kes, you hate those ambulance-chasing weasels."

"They're not all ambulance chasers, Drew. Some attorneys represent those who cannot speak for themselves, those who have no voice in the system, the poor, children, the elderly. Besides, to be practical, there's money in law."

"Okay, I can understand you wanting to help people from a different perspective, and that's cool and everything, but since when have you ever cared about making money?"

"I have to grow up. Ted has child support payments."

Drew rammed his hands in his pockets, his fingers clenched next to the ring box. "Does Ted make you happy?"

"Marvelously happy. He's like Marco Polo, always looking for the next great adventure. He wants us to explore a threesome. Interested?"

Drew thought he might puke. Right there on the sidewalk, in front of their favorite ice cream store, surrounded by kiddies and doting parents, he thought he might upchuck the contents of his stomach.

A threesome. How did Kes think she'd ever have a future with a man only looking for a good time? And how come the conversation had shifted gears so fast from her change of career path to her fucking around? What did one have to do with the other?

Kes had never fooled around. She was solid. Had always known what was bullshit and what was real. What was going on with her? Why the big transformation in her life, in her outlook? What wasn't she telling him? And why wasn't she telling him?

Something in her eyes pulled at his heart. His sweetheart was hurting, and he had to get to the bottom of it.

His throat worked. "Kes, do you really think a threesome will make whatever is bothering you disappear?"

"Nothing is bothering me. Now, if you'll excuse me? I really do need to clear out my desk so I can see Ted tonight."

And with that, the woman he loved walked away, leaving him alone with a ring puckering his pocket and an unsaid proposal loitering on his lips.

Chapter Twenty-Four

That evening, after going out to dinner and then seeing a movie, Kesley invited Ted upstairs to her third floor apartment for the standard après-date cup of coffee.

She never made it to the kitchen to put the pot onto perk. Taking her hand, Ted detoured her into the bedroom.

Once inside, he kissed her.

Not his fault that the brush of his lips made her yearn for more, that her heart remained uninvolved. Nor could she fault his smooth groping, though his touch left her cold. As to their different mindsets—if his suggestion of a threesome seemed inappropriate, when considering the newness of their relationship, well appropriateness had always been the bane of her existence. Hadn't she been trying to shed that nasty character flaw?

Still, she couldn't help but feel that Ted should have waited until *they'd* had sex, just the two of them alone, before mentioning a ménage à trois. She hadn't even gotten naked with him yet—

Tonight, apparently, they would take off the wraps.

She'd been expecting him to make his move. In preparation, Kesley had glammed it up, doing the hair thing and the waxing thing and the new clothes thing before the unveiling. Not easy taking it all off for the first time, harder than hell before a man one barely knows. She'd wanted to look her best.

Frankly, having sex after only two dates felt weird. Weirder still that she was about to sleep with someone before exchanging essential information, like favorite ice cream flavors. But she had to do *something* to get her mind from constantly straying to Drew. Maybe second date sex would stop her terrible cold-turkey withdrawal pains—

Seeing Drew today, outside their old ice cream haunt, brought the pain of losing him to the surface all over again. Tired of feeling professionally ineffective, tired of feeling like a big fat zero in her personal life too, just plain tired, why not look to sex as a quick fix to get her over the hump of losing Drew?

Ted wasn't a bad sort. Not really. Most likely, he'd only suggested a threesome because he thought everyone else was doing them. After fifteen years of marriage, he probably also thought he had a lot of catching up to do. Ted wanted to make up for the lost time spent with his ex, and she wanted to forget all the good times spent with Drew. *Even use*, Kesley mused with a sigh.

After the inoffensive kiss, Ted felt up her breasts some more and she sighed some more, her nipples peaking in half-hearted arousal, her less than enthusiastic responsiveness causing her to pull back.

Now or never, Kesley. "Ted, there's something I need to ask."

"Not to worry, I brought the condoms—with ribs, for a woman's utmost satisfaction."

"Er—how considerate. But that wasn't my question. Ted, what's your favorite ice cream flavor?"

"Never touch desserts, myself." He slapped his relatively flat mid-section. "Gotta watch the old waistline." He walked to the right side of the bed—the side he had probably slept on during marriage—and began to undress. She disrobed on the left, presumably his former wife's side.

Difficult to break old patterns. Modifying established modes of behavior required a concerted effort, a great deal of courage and motivation, and a genuine willingness to try something new. Change took guts—

And Drew had pulled it off with class and grace.

He'd bought a car, was in the process of buying a house, had shifted his career focus...

And dumped her, the stale leftover from his college days.

To be fair, he had called several times and had even arranged to meet with her today. Letting her down easy, she supposed.

And that was quite enough obsessing about Drew.

In order for her to move on, she mustn't think about him. Especially not now, not when she was about to go to bed with another man. Taking a leaf from her first lover's book, she would concentrate on the future.

Was Ted her future?

He was checking her out. When she dropped her bra and panties, his penis levitated quite nicely.

She *so* didn't have penis envy. If she had a penis, it would have been embarrassingly limp. With men, everything was on the outside where a partner could see. Bad enough her vagina was dry, a circumstance Ted was bound to discover during foreplay.

Two minutes later in bed, her lack of vaginal lubrication remained her little secret. Condom in place Ted was ready to go.

Not into her he wasn't!

"Uh…Ted," she began, both hands on his shoulders, fending him off, "maybe you haven't noticed but—Wait!"

She wanted to do this, she did, she *really* did, but she needed more prep time. A few measly boob tweaks did not constitute foreplay. And Ted either hadn't noticed or he just didn't care.

Drew had cared.

Over and above the call of duty, he had cared. She'd assumed all men were like Drew, that they used words and touch to excite a lover. Obviously, Drew was not like all men.

Or, at least, Drew differed tremendously from Ted.

The time they had spent together making love had been both sublime and dirty. Sometimes at the same time. The combination had excited her. Anticipation had her clawing the sheets.

And him.

Louisa Trent

She was surprised she hadn't drawn blood, the way she had gone at that man's back. She was surprised she hadn't worn the sheen right off his remarkably long and thick and obliging—

Mustn't think about that now, not while in bed with another man.

Too late. While thinking about what she and Drew had done together in bed—and not in bed—her nipples hardened and jutted, her vagina moistened.

Bingo! Now, they were talking. This wild anticipation was what great sex was all about.

Unfortunately, Ted hadn't inspired her heated arousal.

Remembering Drew had initiated her hot flush of excitement.

My, my, my But that man had some kind of *fine* hands on him. Sneaky, sneaky hands. And gifted fingers that could make a woman scream.

The memory made her wet. Now if only she could somehow transfer those pleasurable sensations from the memory of Drew to the reality of Ted, she'd be wearing an ear-to-ear grin.

Drew had made her grin in bed. Drew had made her giggle in bed until her sides hurt, and then he would do this tricky thing with his…

Nope. Mustn't go there either.

"Could we get better acquainted first?" she asked Ted.

Ted didn't seem to hear. Why did this selective inattention not surprise her?

As a penis batted her upper thigh, she tapped its owner on the shoulder. "Ted, I don't mean to interrupt, but could we possibly do something else first? You know, preliminaries?"

"Don't need 'em," he boasted.

"But I do," she said, and gave him a shove.

"W-w-what?"

She spelled it out for him. "I said N-O."

Ashen-faced, Ted fell back onto the pillows.

Once out from under him, Kesley swung her legs over the edge of the bed and stood.

She could have taken the path of least resistance, pretended Ted was Drew, but substituting one lover for another in her thoughts amounted to sexual dishonesty and made her feel like a cheat. Far more honest to admit she'd made a dreadful mistake and then ask No-Foreplay Ted to leave. And if he didn't see things quite that way, her knee would instruct him in the protocol of bedroom etiquette.

Kesley belted her new sexy black satin robe in place. Modestly covered from throat to thigh, she felt more in charge, more in control…less irritated with Ted.

She shouldn't take out her frustration and disappointment on him. So Ted wasn't the world's greatest lover—she could have invested the time and shown him what turned her on in bed. But poor attention to details wasn't Ted's major failing.

Ted wasn't Drew, and no amount of coaching on her part would alter that circumstance.

"Ted, I think you should…"

Rattling door hinges interrupted her goodbye speech.

The man who had spent a decade on foreplay with her, who understood the ins and outs of her woman's body in the dark, by candlelight, when she was vertical, horizontal, and yes, on all fours too, stood at the threshold to her bedroom, no slouch to be seen anywhere in his posture.

"I've decided to accept your threesome invitation after all," he said.

Chapter Twenty-Five

Drew reached out a hand to the little fuck in the bed. "Andrew."

"Ted," replied the little fuck.

They shook on it.

Amenities observed, Drew went for his belt buckle.

His equanimity?

All-show. He hated seeing Kes with another guy, hated the idea of her sharing herself with anyone but him. The same sick feeling that had overtaken him outside the ice cream shop earlier that day threatened again. One thing for a man to empty the contents of his stomach in privacy, another while trying to act all cool and calm and civilized to impress his woman. Puking was not real suave.

Neither was pummeling the little fuck to within an inch of his life.

Kes wouldn't go for that kind of behavior. But that kind of behavior had always been second nature to him—

Until he'd met a college girl with stars shining in her eyes.

After meeting Kes, he'd cleaned up his act, stopped making his way with his fists. There was no big secret to his turn around. It all came down to love. When you loved someone, as he loved Kes, a man walked the straight and narrow.

For Kes, he had made something of himself, so she'd be proud of him. For Kes, he had stayed out of jail and resisted the allure of an early coffin.

Damn straight, before meeting her, he'd been headed to the first location and then to the other. He'd known it. Everyone around him had known it. College had only been a small detour on the way to going nowhere.

He'd always loved to read, and he wasn't a dummy. Even after growing up on the streets, he'd gotten into college. But he wouldn't have stayed there, wouldn't have lasted, never would have graduated, if not for Kes.

He'd been on academic probation, on the verge of flunking out, the year he'd moved into the three-decker. After meeting Kes, he'd worked his ass off to pull his grades up so he could stay in school.

Going from nothing to someone hadn't happened overnight. Fact was, he still had to work at it—as evidenced by his first impulse, which was to beat the opportunistic Ted to a bloody pulp.

The little fuck wasn't worth the aggravation of an assault rap. Kes didn't love Ted. Kes loved him, Drew, the former street kid who was holding her eyes with everything he had inside him while hanging his clothes on the floor.

As naked as he'd ever been to anyone, he took his sweetheart's lips.

They clung.

Drew sighed his relief into the kiss. Then, ignoring Ted, slid his tongue home, a welcome he'd dreamt about for a decade—

No, that wasn't right. Not for only decade. All of his life.

He broke the kiss, but only temporarily—Kes liked lots of kissing during lovemaking and Drew happily obliged, because kissing Kes was making love.

"Better get in under the covers, sweetheart, so you don't get chilled." He flipped back the covers for her, and shot a warning look at the occupant already in the bed. "Leave on the robe."

Ted on the right side of the mattress, Drew taking up the left, Kes sandwiched in the middle, staring at the ceiling.

"I don't know what to do," she said, sounding dazed.

Drew knew. He knew exactly what to do. There were too many damn cocks in the bed and he was getting rid of one of them.

"I'll do whatever you want. Lady's choice," he said solemnly.

"I would like you to touch me." Her lids lowered.

Over the robe, Drew cupped his sweetheart's pretty breast. Delivered a look to kill at Ted.

"Mmm," Kes murmured.

"Yeah," Drew groaned in agreement.

Ted knew enough to keep his damn mouth shut.

Sex could get downright confusing, Drew mused.

Sometimes people made incredibly stupid mistakes. Mistakes made, maybe because, when it came right down to it, sex was less about bodies than about the other stuff—trust and love and emotional bonds—the intangibles that might, if a guy got lucky, convince a beautiful woman to forgive his inexcusable feet dragging.

He'd made plenty of mistakes in the past, but he wasn't about to make one now. Now he was sure, as sure as he'd never been before. He was moving forward. With Kes.

Drew turned to the little fuck. "Get lost, Ted."

As Ted wisely left the room, Drew spoke the words too long in coming. "I love you, sweetheart. You're my whole life."

Her eyes snapped open. "How dare you say that to me!"

Moving forward wasn't always easy. "I dare, because you told me I snored."

"What?" She got up on her elbows.

"You told me I snored. Like a bear in hibernation. You told me yourself, only a woman who loves a man would tell him something uncomplimentary like that. You love me, Kes."

She pounced. Straddling him, she popped him one right between the eyes.

Sometimes, Drew conceded, the intangibles could get messy. The occasional nosebleed came with the territory.

He quick sniffed before he dotted the bed sheets red. "When you're done pummeling me, sweetheart, we're talking."

For a lightweight, Kes had a mean right hook. And no argument, he had the slugfest coming. But when her punches grew sloppy and her breathing went choppy, Drew knew he had to end it. "Quit now, baby," he crooned. "You're getting all worn out."

Kes, not seeing things quite the same way, kept the punches flying.

The woman had the tenacity of a bulldog. She'd stuck with him for ten years, long after another woman would have packed it all in and given up.

Not his sweetheart. Kes didn't know the meaning of the word quit. She'd keep at him until she collapsed in exhaustion.

There was only one thing for him to do.

Grabbing hold of her wrists in one hand, Drew rolled Kes beneath him and kneed open her robe-covered thighs.

Time to turn intangible into tangible. "My cock is going in you."

"You bastard!"

He laughed. "Got that right. Never knew my mother or my father. The only person I've ever really belonged to is you. Now let me in."

"Wh-what?"

"I love you," he said, voice weak, dick as firm as his resolve not to lose her. "I love you with everything I've got to love another human being with. I wasn't sure if that was gonna be enough, but it's all I got, and it's yours."

In her concern for him, his compassionate sweetheart quit her struggling and settled down, and he immediately let go of her wrists.

Just as he knew would happen, her social worker's instinct's kicked in. "Your parents didn't raise you?"

"Nope. Never made their acquaintance. You know those kids you work with at The Shelter? A few years back, in a different state, I was one of them."

Tears drained down her face. "Why didn't you tell me? It would have explained so much. Your inability to stay with one love interest..."

"I stayed with you, goddammit And those tears on your face are the reason I didn't want to tell you. I didn't want to be just a case study to you.

-211-

Poor neglected Drew, another homeless teen living on the streets—working the streets. Blah, blah, blah. Cry me a river."

He sucked in some air. "I'm so over my early years. I'm a successful man, and that's how I wanted you to see me. And you know something? Much of that success I owe to *you. You* gave me stability. I fucked around but I always returned to *you.*"

She gurgled out a half-sob, half-hiccup. "Oh, sure, you returned to me. You lived downstairs."

"I'm worth a mint, sweetheart. My business is booming. I could have moved out of this rat-infested three-decker the first year after I graduated college, but that would have taken me away from you. I didn't know if I could give you the love you deserved, but I sure as hell knew that wherever you were, that's where I wanted to be."

She shook her head. "You give me too much credit. You made something out of yourself, all by yourself. I had nothing to do with any of it."

He nipped that line of reasoning right in the bud. "You had everything to do with it. I was only just now thinking how you turned me around. You do the same motivating routine down at The Shelter. Those runaways listen to you."

"Not all of them." Kes started sobbing. "There's a kid…"

A kid.

Not a kid, THE KID was more like it. The one Kes had been so worried about. The one she wouldn't talk to him about. "What's his name?"

"He went by the name of John Smith. But that was an alias. I can't violate his confidentiality by telling you the circumstances surrounding his running, but they were just so sad. He had so much potential. With just a little support, he could easily have been mainstreamed. But he took off. Refused to enter any programs at The Shelter. He was a good kid, with a horrible tragedy in his life, and I failed him."

"You didn't fail him. He just wasn't ready to listen. I'm telling you, if not for your little pep talks, if not for you always riding my ass, I would have dropped out of college." So hard to talk about the past, but for Kes, he forced the words out. "You want to save someone? Okay, here it is. *You fucking saved me* Sometimes, you can't save the whole world at once, sweetheart. Sometimes, saving the world only happens one person at a time."

"Oh, Drew." She pulled him close. "I love you so much. What would I ever do without you?"

"I'm never giving you the chance to find out. Marry me."

Drew paused, got himself under control. This was Kes he was proposing to, and he intended on taking his time, and doing things the right way. "That is, marry me after we go visit your parents and I ask your dad's permission. Then, I want you to marry me."

"Yes, I'll marry you. But first I need to tell you about Ted…"

"Fuck Ted."

"That's what I need to tell you—I didn't. I only invited him over tonight to help me get over you. Rebounding, you know? But I couldn't go through with it. I was about to ask him to leave, when you arrived."

"You're with me now and you'll be with me in the future. All that other stuff is in the past, and as far as I'm concerned, the past stays in the past. It wouldn't have mattered to me, even if you had fucked him up the ass sideways…"

"I think that would have been anatomically impossible." She snorted. Then started to giggle. Then whooped with belly laughs.

"Man, do you have a lot to learn about sex toys. I can see I'm gonna have to buy you a strap-on for the honeymoon."

Guffawing right along with her now, tears streaming down his face too, Drew pulled Kes tight against his heart.

Christ, but he loved this woman. So much so, he didn't even mind losing his hard-on in the resultant hysteria. What the hell. They had the rest of their lives ahead of them to make love.

Just being with his sweetheart was perfect.

About the Author

Louisa Trent is happiest writing and so she writes all the time, even when the veggies are in need of peeling and the dust bunnies are in need of vacuuming. When she was far too young to contemplate anything as serious as marriage, she snatched up a boy with a sense of humor and led him straight to the altar. Somewhere along the way, she picked up a couple of academic degrees, which she uses every day, only not in the way she intended to use them. Blessed with three funny sons and a husband who still makes her giggle, she lives in a quaint New England town, in a messy home, surrounded by flowers and laughter.

Visit with Louisa at www.louisatrent.com or email her at louisatrent@louisatrent.com

Sometimes fate-and mothers-can ruin the best-laid plans.

Settling The Score
© *2006 Elisa Adams*

At thirty-one, Jake Storm is happy with his life the way it is. He has a great job, a nice apartment, and plenty of free time to do as he pleases. Settling down isn't even an option. Too bad his meddling mother doesn't understand that.

Amber Velez has a reputation—but not the good kind. In high school, she was the nerd. The overweight, four-eyed geek everyone picked on. Now she's back in town, with a whole new look and a whole new attitude, and she's ready to show a certain man what he could have had if he hadn't used her and broken her heart.

Jake has lifetime bachelorhood on his mind. Amber has revenge on hers. But fate has other plans.

Warning: This book contains monogamous sex scenes using some graphic language.

Available now in ebook and print from Samhain Publishing.

Enjoy the following excerpt from Settling the Score...

The way Jake saw it, he had two choices. He could either pretend he didn't recognize the woman he'd just about knocked over in his rush to get to a date he didn't even want, or run like hell in the other direction. Out of the two choices, neither seemed particularly reasonable, but running held a lot of appeal.

At that moment, as he looked into familiar green eyes and caught more than a hint of humor, all the chatter in the restaurant faded to a dull roar. The music, the laughter, the clang of plates and flatware all disappeared, leaving him standing alone against the one woman he'd hoped to never see again. The only woman who'd ever been able to get under his skin and turn him inside out.

Why now? Why here, of all places? If he didn't know any better, he'd think his mother set the whole thing up, but even she wasn't that devious. He hoped.

"Hi, Jake." Amber's smooth, smoky voice rolled over him like a caress. A caress he felt everywhere. In the thirteen years since he'd last seen her, he hadn't forgotten that voice. Back in high school, it had been a voice that didn't fit her body. It fit now. Too well. It took him a few seconds to recover the power of speech.

"Hi."

Bumbling idiot that he'd suddenly become, he couldn't manage more than a single, lame word in response to what remained unspoken between them. All he could do was stare at the woman she'd become and wonder what had happened to the shy, overweight girl he'd known for most of his life. The one who'd hidden behind thick, plastic-framed glasses, bulky sweaters, and science-club meetings. Her voice was the same. Her eyes too. But everything else had changed.

He'd known about her transformation—couldn't have missed hearing about it, given that his mother and hers were best friends and two of the biggest busybodies in town—but some part of him had refused to believe it until this moment, when he'd actually gotten a chance to see what they'd been talking about. Now the woman who'd always tried her hardest to fade into the background practically screamed "notice me" without having to say a word. He'd noticed. Taken inventory of every inch of her.

"How have you been?" she continued, humor glinting in those big green eyes. She smelled like flowers and some sort of exotic spice. It hit him like a punch in the gut and stirred parts of his body he tried to will to remain dormant. The last thing he needed right now was a hard-on. She'd slap him for sure.

"Jake?" Her husky laugh alerted him to the fact that he had yet to answer her question.

"I...uh...I'm good." Good? Freakin' stupid response, moron. Anything else you'd like to do to make a fool of yourself? All those years at Harvard, and he was reduced to an incoherent idiot when faced with a beautiful woman.

No. Not just any beautiful woman. He'd dated his fair share of them, and none had ever affected him the way Amber was tonight. There was something about her that made his brain threaten to shut down. He cleared his throat. "How have you been?"

"I've been great. It's good to see you."

It was more than good to see her. The second their bodies had touched, every single one of his nerves had stood up and taken notice. Yet another hazard of running smack into a beautiful, curvy woman.

She was beautiful, too. In a way he never would have imagined. All lean lines and gentle curves. Even her hair had changed. What used to be a long, frizzy mess had turned into shiny curls the color of black coffee. Her natural color, he knew, and it complemented the rich, warm tones of her caramel skin. The curls fell to just below her shoulders and made him want to tangle his fingers in them to see if they were really as soft as they looked.

Her dress was red. Short and tight enough to afford him a good look at her nipped waist above slightly flared hips. Cut low enough that it revealed a mouth-watering amount of cleavage. She had to be wearing heels—four-inchers, since the top of her head was at his eye level. Shit. He loved a woman in heels. The higher the better. Maybe it was a little shallow, but he'd always been a visual kind of guy.

Spiked heels and a red dress. Guaranteed to make him go rock-solid in seconds flat. He swallowed hard. Here he was, meeting another woman for a blind date he'd rather avoid, and all he could think about was a woman who wouldn't want him.

"You look good, Amber." The words slipped out before he could pull them back, and he muttered a curse. He would not, would not, hit on Amber Velez, no matter how much his body begged. She wouldn't be interested, and even if she was, he didn't deserve a second chance. She'd trusted him once, a long time ago, and he'd trampled on her feelings. She wasn't the kind of woman to forgive a betrayal like that so easily.

Her gaze left his and traveled down his body in a slow perusal that had him clenching his hands into fists. For a woman who shouldn't be interested, she certainly didn't act the part. By the time her gaze came back to his, he couldn't stand still.

What would you do?

Trophy Girl
© *2006 Melani Blazer*

You're a NASCAR fan...pretty into it, thanks to your dad. You know a lot about the drivers, the tracks, the cars. Even though you try not to, you hear the rumors and see the off-track interviews. You know the reputation of the series champ, bad-boy Zander Torris. You know he's devastatingly good looking, and charming to boot, but with a different piece of voluptuous, blonde eye candy on his arm every weekend, you have zilch respect for him.

The only good thing you see in him is that he's a very generous benefactor for the camp where you're a nurse volunteer.

So when he walks into your clinic, unannounced and unexpected, and asks you—girl-next-door, unglamorous you—to that evening's benefactor's dinner, what do you do?

Hint, he's not taking no for an answer, so be ready at 6...

Warning, this title contains the following: explicit sex and graphic language.

Available now in ebook and print from Samhain Publishing.

Enjoy the following excerpt Trophy Girl...

The media were already lining up behind his SUV when Zander got out of the vehicle in the hotel parking lot. He should talk to them, toss out promo for the camp and the brand new "Dream Come True" foundation he would be donating his time to. But he knew they didn't want to hear that. No, they were more interested in the rumors about his car chief, if his sponsor had signed on again for next year and if the recent lull in his "public" private life had anything to do with his lackluster performance on the track. He'd burned that article. And the one suggesting he was gay. Okay, that one had actually made him laugh. All these years his sexual preference had never been questioned and he went one weekend at the track without a female presence and suddenly he had jumped the fence.

Pasting on a practiced and very fake smile, he waved at the hated flashbulbs and ducked into the lobby. Could it be worse if he were a movie star? All he wanted to do was drive, dammit. That's where he worked best, all strapped in to a seven hundred plus horsepower drive machine and let loose with forty of the world's best drivers. Let someone else handle all this media shit. He was tired of defending his personal life—most of it focusing on his love life. Pretty funny considering he didn't even have one. He'd tried a relationship, with more than disastrous results. Never again. Never.

He shot his hand through his hair and thanked his lucky stars the elevator was empty.

Room four-twenty. He paused with his fist poised just beneath the number. He was early, but was taking no chances. He'd asked her on a whim. Wasn't something he'd planned until the words were out of his mouth. She was the polar opposite of what the media seemed to like to pair him with. Plenty attractive in a wholesome way, clearly intelligent and hey, she spent her vacation volunteering for kids. He dared the media to say something bad about that.

When he knocked and she answered the door completely ready, he smiled. Perfect. He knew she'd be there, and had guessed she'd be dressed professionally. Boring.

"You look…nice," he said, noting the harsh black pantsuit she wore at least outlined her very shapely figure. With a little wardrobe help, she'd look stunning on his arm. That should sell some papers.

She winced and smoothed her hands over her hips. "You're early."

"You're ready. Besides, I've got a stop to make first." He gave her his best half-grin and waited.

Molly's shoulders rose and fell, then she closed the door on him. His smile erupted and he let out a chuckle. Damn, this was going to be fun.

"I'd really prefer to drive," she informed him as she emerged from the room a moment later and ducked under his arm. She headed straight for the elevator without slowing down. "I wish I'd known how to reach you earlier and I would have told you that."

He lifted an eyebrow. Was she afraid of him? Why else did she dart away like he might harm her? "I don't think so, Miss Molly. Can you imagine how the media would have a field day with that?"

"You asked me to come to give a report on the kids, not make you look good in print," she reminded him.

He eyed her up and down, enjoying the flash of fire in her. Much better than the gold diggers who seemed to be hot on his heels at every venue he visited.

"Let's compromise here." Zander leaned in as they boarded the elevator. She wore a sinful scent, one that filled his mind with images of black lace, creamy skin and sex. Damn, she smelled delicious. She stood facing straight ahead on the other side of the small space. Moving closer, intentionally too close for her to remain comfortable, he spoke barely above a whisper. "I'll feed you if you pretend you enjoy my company. You'll get to sing praises to the board, they'll continue to think the camp is a brilliant idea, all will be great."

She crossed her arms over her chest, but he could see her chest rising and falling unevenly. So she wasn't unaffected!

"And you'll get the benefit of having a single woman on your arm."

"Thank God you're single. I'd hate to have to beat up a jealous husband."

She snorted, then frowned at him, causing her smooth forehead to wrinkle. "You're incorrigible."

"But you'll do it?"

He didn't worry that she didn't answer. Meant she was thinking about it.

"You drove, eh?" she commented when he led her up to the dark SUV.

"I am a driver." Did she really need reminding? And no way was he going to have someone cart him around. He dealt with enough of that at the track. Hell, they didn't even let him drive his own golf cart to and from his trailer.

"Yeah, I know that," she replied, pursing those perfectly painted lips in a show of impatience. She even ignored his hand as he offered to help her climb up into his truck. Okay, her rebellion was starting to get old. She could at least be polite.

He got in his side. "Are you really angry with me about this whole thing?" He doubted it—she had been ready to go.

"I'm here aren't I?" she slung back, then shook her head and turned sideways as he buckled his seat belt and lowered the tilt wheel. "But then, you probably think I came because you're famous."

"Didn't you?"

"No," she retorted, leaning back in the seat and crossing her arms over her chest. She couldn't possibly realize the scowl brought color to her cheeks and the way she pushed against her chest made her enticing cleavage a little more visible. "Though you could have warned me about the camera crew you'd brought along." She waved out the window at the sporadic pops of the bright flashes.

"They're annoying as hell and there'll be plenty more at the dinner. But back to you—I'm a bit surprised you came without more of a fight. You're just jumping in a vehicle with a stranger and—"

"Oh please. Zander, you know damn well you had the advantage of your fame—yes, I know who you are and what you do, but I'm not interested in a relationship, sex, or your damn money."

"Who said anything about sex?" He didn't hide his smile. Any minute now, there'd be smoke rising from her ears.

"Just drive, dammit. Drive."

"I can do that," he said. But that conversation was far from over. Far from over. He was dying to ask why she'd come, since she'd adamantly denied all the logical reasons. He'd pissed her off. Damn, she was cute when she pouted.

She kept her eyes averted. That was just fine with him. It gave him the chance to really study her features. She had a great profile, strong, yet feminine all at once. She was too pale—the girl clearly needed to get out in the sun more, but somehow the contrast with her near black hair and dark blue eyes made her—not pretty, no, she was past pretty. She wasn't necessarily glamorous either—he'd seen too many of those mask wearing females whose appearance was shallow. Molly had a glow about her, making her almost untouchable. Well, no, that wasn't quite what he was thinking, either.

Shit. He hit the brakes and swerved to miss the car in front of him whose driver had decided to turn without a signal. "Bastard," he muttered. Glancing over at Molly, he growled at the amused lift of her eyebrows and the corner of her mouth.

"Where are you going in such a hurry?" she asked. "It's not 'til seven, right?"

He tightened his grip on the steering wheel and refused to look over at her. She was damn distracting and the last thing he wanted was the humiliation of a car accident. Those were bad enough on track, where they were usually acceptable. "I need to do a bit of shopping."

Zander had made a few inquiries at the front desk of the hotel, learning the location of the best women's dress store in town, then made a call. When he parked in front of the upscale boutique, Molly didn't say a word. Neither did she budge from her arms-over-chest, eyes-straight-ahead pose.

"You getting out, or do you trust me enough to do this on my own?" he teased.

"What?"

"Sweetheart, you look nice and all, but that's not nearly what I had in mind for you to be wearing tonight." Damn, she was gonna go ballistic, he just knew it. And his groin tightened in anticipation. So maybe he did have a death wish. He loved controversy, courted it constantly. But never had pissing off a cameraman been as much fun as this.

Samhain Publishing, Ltd.

It's all about the story…

Action/Adventure
Fantasy
Historical
Horror
Mainstream
Mystery/Suspense
Non-Fiction
Paranormal
Red Hots!
Romance
Science Fiction
Western
Young Adult

http://www.samhainpublishing.com

Printed in the United States
59833LVS00004B/1-273

9 781599 982779